"SKIN SLUT"
A SPLATTER NOVELLA

"SKIN SLUT"
A SPLATTER NOVELLA

FINN VANDERGRIFT
& REGINA WATTS

PAINTED BLIND
PUBLISHING
LITERARY ALCHEMY

PAINTED BLIND
PUBLISHING
LITERARY ALCHEMY

01

The yearning began right around her birthday. She met a boy her age, a year older, at a local park one summer afternoon. He seemed so perfect for her—a good Catholic boy whose parents were devout Catholics, just like hers. They met at one of Daddy's philanthropic obligations and hit it off right away when they found out they were going to the same college. He didn't even mind that Erica was taking her classes while living at home instead of staying in the dorm; at the very least, he never had a chance to ask her why.

The day he picked her up in his slightly dented Mercedes, she had butterflies. Wasn't it nice to have a little attention?

His name was Brad. They talked about school, about music, about his part-time job at the park. He made her laugh, which she did to make people more comfortable. Erica had never been able to get any guy to warm up to her that easily. This boy had an easy confidence she'd never seen in anyone before. She wanted to impress him, and he clearly wanted to impress her. He'd endangered his job by taking her to the shut-down park visitors' center, because it was the only place private enough to talk.

She undid her jeans and showed him how she masturbated to fantasies. Fantasies, mind! What was more harmless than a fantasy? Erica had a lot of them, constructed in vivid detail while reading her favorite porn magazines in her father's collection of first-wave cannibal erotica, back from '99 when the overpopulation lobbyists finally legalized consensual cannibalism without fully thinking through what kind of legislation would be required to moderate its porn industry. That was when the good stuff, the real stuff with real victims, was still being published—none of this phony volunteer shit where everything had to be consensual and contracted. She made herself squirm as she told Brad exactly which fantasies turned her on and why they excited her. She even described some of the gore-riddled sex scenes she fantasized about the most.

By Erica's day in '23, cannibalism was considered an undesirable and dangerous lifestyle choice, but a public service and a tolerated form of harm reduction. Why, non-consensual murder had dropped by something like 60% in the first years after the legislation. Cannibalism was downright normal: practically institutionalized. Therefore, when it came to telling Brad about her dirty little daydreams of humping some dead guy's intestinal tract, Erica thought he'd get excited and make out with her; maybe take out his dick and try to put it in.

He did not react like that. Instead, he stared at her breasts with this odd expression on his face, as though he were trying to use the sight of them to blot out her words. Dissociating, basically. He was looking at her tits with a kind of shock, his eyes fixed on the same spot for what felt like a long time before he managed to tear his gaze away to her face. And then, he stopped her mid-sentence.

"What the fuck is the matter with you, Erica?"

Erica stopped moving and just sat there in silence. Then, Brad laughed.

Erica didn't understand. But when he laughed again, she felt something snap inside her. What the hell was this idiot's problem? Didn't he know anything? Didn't he know kink-shaming was something only done by rude, out-of-touch hillbillies? Her rage and shame and pain were writhing within her like a shaken can of soda, and it seemed like every last drop of that fury was about to foam out.

"What the fuck is the matter with *me*? More like what the hell's wrong with you, Brad? What's so fucking funny, exactly?"

After jerking on her shorts, she stood up abruptly and yanked open the visitors' center door. In the parking lot, while he stood there struggling to lock the building, Erica screamed in his face and slapped him until blood came pouring out of his nose. She'd never felt such anger and couldn't even explain where it was coming from, or what was happening to her: through her. She just knew it felt good to be in such a hideous rage. Like being possessed, maybe, and therefore liberated from all responsibility.

It was all happening so fast that Brad didn't know what to say or do. He just stood there with his hands raised and his mouth open dumbly, the bovine look in his eyes somewhat baffled rather than outraged. When he tried to walk away, she grabbed his cheap necktie and he struggled against her until, by complete accident, she fell onto the asphalt. She began screaming again, louder than ever.

Erica got up on her feet with another grab at his tie. Brad sprinted toward the car without looking back, but she was quicker and tackled him as he reached the pavement. His head smashed into the hard asphalt. Brad's face twisted and blood began spilling from his nose and mouth. Erica took his necktie off. Brad gasped for air, trying to get her off him, but Erica kept him pinned with her knees pinned to either side of his chest. She wrapped the tie around his throat and pulled it tight enough for his breathing to become impossible. The surge of power was so irresistible—so hot!—that, almost without thinking, she leaned down and kissed him right on the lips. Erica sucked on his tongue as it came into contact with hers, marveling at how quickly it swelled to the shape of a fat garden slug.

Brad looked into her eyes with a strange expression. He tried to speak to her but couldn't make any noise:

nothing but a wheezing rasp, as if his lungs were full of cement. He couldn't even gasp for air. He tried to grab her hair, but she slapped his hands away. Erica held his wrists firmly with one hand while using the other to throttle his necktie. The blood running from his nose and mouth had somehow stained her hand. She licked the blood off her finger as his body went limp beneath her and, in a frenzy, she rocked her hips to grind herself against his chest. It was mere seconds before an electric bolt of pleasure struck her head to toe.

The pressure eased, internally and externally. Everything went so still. Erica smiled at Brad: a warm, pleased smile, as the mother gives the infant who has finally stopped crying and given in to sleep. She sat on top of his corpse for several seconds, admiring his perfect body with her first cogent thought—"What a waste!"—rising in her mind as she removed her phone from her pocket. White flashes lit the parking lot, bouncing off his Mercedes to add to her brief spells of blindness as she snapped pictures of the bloodied cadaver. Then, realizing she was sitting on top of a corpse—an illegal corpse, being the product of non-consensual homicide—Erica scrambled up to assess the situation. The night was dark, and the little city park was too cheap for cameras. Nobody was around, either: she looked up and down the street before walking to the nearest bus stop.

That night, after she told her mother she'd had a nice date and would put herself to bed, Erica stood behind the door of her bedroom and remembered every orgiastic second of Brad's death. It felt so good to watch him die; and the uncontrollable, wild way his life had ended because of her rage—no, because he had deserved it for making fun of her—made it even better than she could have imagined. There was no reason or logic to why that was so. She just knew that her pleasure was so much greater to think he died for spurning her. Her body quivered again at the memory of the orgasm she'd had right after he was killed. It was amazing how good an orgasm felt when you were in a bad mood and desperate for some relief, and this was even better than normal because it was the climax of a fantasy—the climax of her entire life, or maybe only the true beginning. She wondered if the thrill would ever get old. Could it always feel as good as this?

Erica squirmed, desperate to relive the day. She scrolled through her photos on her phone, hot all over again to see Brad's dead mouth open and deformed with stagnant blood. She wished she had taken a video, damn it...but maybe she could do that next time, if she ever had another chance. She sensed that she would, somehow: moreover, she couldn't help feeling that the odds of anyone linking her to Brad's murder was low. Her family just wasn't known for that sort of thing. The cops probably wouldn't even worry about checking her phone, if they were smart enough to find out she'd been on a date with the boy the night of his death. This was Erica they would be talking about: sweet, innocent, wholesome Erica, middle-class suburbia made manifest as a human girl. Could anyone really think that she was the sort of girl who'd rather gnaw on a guy's cock than take it in her cunt?

Now that was what really sounded like fun. Sure, sure—non-consensual homicide was all well and fun. She had never seen a dead body before, and she wondered why she hadn't tried murder sooner. But eating human flesh? Tasting some screaming boy's offal while she fucked him with a knife? Now that was recreation. It wasn't even a question of legality, as long as the paperwork was in order. Overpopulation and its impact on the climate was statistically more deadly than the likelihood one's son or daughter would become embroiled in cannibalism. She knew from reading advice columns in her father's porn magazines that consensual cannibals were persecuted, even when they avoided videos where anyone actually died.

And by means of these columns, it turned out that there were a lot of women who liked this stuff just like Erica did. They called themselves "skinsluts," which was the same name as one of her dad's most meticulously collected rags. When Erica came home from classes at her college the next day to a house still empty, she scoured the newest editions she could find and pieced together that these skinsluts existed in the underground culture as a kind of society, helping one another to hedonistically butchering and eat men and women as part of sex play. An old website the magazine listed no longer existed, but she managed to locate a discussion forum full of users reminiscing about the old site. After browsing it well into the night, Erica decided to get in touch with the local skinslut community to find out what she could learn about eating a guy like Brad (call him, Brad 2.0) without the subsequent hassle of a police investigation, but she didn't even know where skinsluts hung out in real life. She thought it might be a good idea to contact an older skin—a woman in her 30s—and get her advice for first time experiences like this. Like a mentor. But how to get that far? Erica plunged deep into the belly of the Internet, scouring communities and researching long-since abandoned pages.

Then, she discovered the website for Bazaar.

It was sparse. Very sparse, with a black background and off-white text beneath the sumptuous curves of the glossy logo.

Into skin?
Inquire within.
Have some doubt?
Then keep out.

Aside from the weird little ditty, there was absolutely nothing else she could note. The site had come up in the first place thanks to a surprisingly difficult dive into a sketchy personal ad website, where freelance cannibal enthusiasts posted looking for volunteers. Erica pulled the ad that had caught her eye again.

Live your last days in pleasure
(Serious inquiries only)

Bazaar is a private club for adventurous, like-minded fleshies and skinsluts. You've seen the rest. Now experience the best. Our unique blend of sexuality, dining, and entertainment will leave you wanting more.

Bazaar is a place where you can be yourself. Where you can meet others who understand you. Where you can put your inhibitions to rest and indulge in the pleasures you've been craving.

Bazaar is a place of unconditional acceptance.

Our fleshies receive a generous stipend, and their payout is distributed to their relatives upon their demise.

Bazaar is a place of comfort and security.

Interested? Call us.

It seemed like the ad itself was more professionally written than a lot of the rest of them, promising a pay-out to the intended victim's family, and it offered something they didn't: a phone number.

Erica took a deep breath when the phone's ringing was interrupted by a short, gruff, "Can I help you?"

"Hello," Erica blurted into the receiver, cringing at her own wording but unable to stop herself, "is this a place I can go to meet skinsluts?"

The man who answered sounded surprised when she asked him. He said no, and that he couldn't tell her where that might be. She didn't believe him, but he sounded very sincere. "Listen, kid—I don't know what you're talking about."

"I'm not a kid," she insisted. "And I'm sure you know what I mean. Come on, dude—I saw the ad. Is Tania there?"

A second of hesitation stood before the man's next protest. "There's nobody here by that name," he lied, more weakly now.

Erica scoffed. She left a message with him anyway: her name, her number, and her interest. The man seemed to listen against his better judgment, then said once more, "You're barking up the wrong tree," and hung up on her.

She tried not to be too discouraged. Maybe it would turn out useful.

The guy's name was Gabe. He must have gotten permission from somebody, because a day later he called back and told her the address for Bazaar. She made plans to visit on a Saturday evening, which would mean she could stay out without suspicion if she told her family she was just out seeing friends. When her father dropped her off, however, she was shocked to find it a strip joint! What a relief that she had given him the address of an ice cream parlor six blocks down. The city really was a little more exciting than the suburbs...everything was so close together. She tried not to blush as they drove past, taking in the place's nature from its marquee and windowless façade. Dad was oblivious, reminding her while smoothly slid his car into a place along the curb to call him when she wanted to be picked up.

As soon as he was gone, Erica walked briskly down the sidewalk to the waiting club. She'd worn heels and applied make-up the way her drunk aunt taught her to, babying her and making her into a glamorized little doll. Heavy eyeshadow made girls look like young women, and young women look like fairies, and old women look fresh and alive. When, to Erica's surprise, she got in with the password this Gabe guy had given her, she found there were a lot of older women mingling with the mostly male guests and sometimes watching the dancers. She guessed they were skinsluts. One of them seemed to recognize her at once—Erica recognized her, too, in a way Erica couldn't quite explain. The woman strode up to greet her while she stood uncertainly by the door.

"You must be Erica, right?"

The woman was in her late 40s. Her skin was a little rough, like she wasn't quite so young anymore after years of tanning booths, and there was some gray hair in her brownish black hair—but she was still pretty sexy, sweet-smelling and artfully ornamented with jewels that fell across the cleavage rising from the leopard print top underneath her leather jacket.

And she looked very happy to see Erica, which made Erica a bit nervous.

Trying to keep her voice at a slightly deeper timbre than usual, Erica said, "Yes...I am."

"My name is Tania. Nice to meet you." The woman smiled, extending her hand. On the stage behind her, women a little closer to Erica's age gyrated on the stage in outfits more S&M than traditional "g-string" strip joint. "So...you think you want to be a skinslut, huh?"

Seizing her chance, Erica asked, "I think so, but— What exactly does it mean?"

"A skinslut is someone who likes eating human flesh," Tania said matter-of-factly. "But it's more than that, too. It's a community. We support each other. We connect each other to security and success, and empower each other. Why are you here if you don't know that?"

Erica's cheeks burned with humiliation. "Of course, I know that. But—do you really get a lot of willing men?"

"What man wouldn't want to be eaten by us?"

As Tania gestured around the room, Erica had a whole new perspective on the glazed-over simps being entranced by the dancers. Tania smiled and nodded toward the back of the room, where she had indicated there was an empty booth. She invited Erica to sit next to her, patting the leather seat.

The waitress came over to ask what drinks they'd like to order. When Tania ordered a Long Island Iced Tea for herself, Erica decided she didn't need anything so strong. She asked for a Coke. As the waitress hurried off again, the dental floss in her ass crack drew Erica's eye. At least some things about this place were more like a normal strip club...but the hooks hanging from the ceiling and the shimmering red wallpaper that made the whole place look like pulsating meat were still more than enough to keep Bazaar true to its name.

"Are you ready to get started?" Tania asked.

Erica gulped and nodded. "Yeah...okay."

"Good. Then let me start by telling you how the flesh-eating community works. First, you have to understand this is a family. I really mean it, Erica—we need to operate within careful legal limits if we're not going to wind up penalized. If you're really serious, which we'll see tonight, then you'll be a part of that family, and expected to obey its rules. This is a new life. Every skinslut must have a special name, but for plausible deniability we usually just call each other "skinslut" or "skin"...though, of course, we're just fleshies, too, in the end. You'll hear that a lot around here."

"Why do you need special skinslut names? I thought all this was legal." Erica was still getting used to this new language of sex play, and still reeling with the idea that Tania was speaking with her in such a genuine way. She must have seen something valuable in Erica. Some kind of potential. Bolstered by this thought, Erica went on, "I mean, I see cannibalism in lots of my old man's hardcore magazines these days."

Tania smiled at the mention of her dad's old magazines. "Well...it's illegal to be a real skinslut—

and we are really skinsluts, baby, let me tell you—but it's not illegal to eat a fleshie if he wants to be eaten. And some people do, of course, want to be eaten. But you have to be careful, because most guys who are eaten aren't actually into being eaten...some are, but many aren't. So you don't want to eat someone just 'cuz you like his dick and think you can turn him around to eating. You have to find the right kind of guy. And then there's being eaten, yourself."

Erica frowned. "I'd rather do the eating," she protested while her new mentor smiled on. "Guys are always such predators about it, which is why I think I like the idea of eating one so much. Like, what—do they think eating someone like me turns them into something better than just a human being?"

"It's not about them, honey," Tania said. "The men who do the eating themselves do so because of their attraction to women who they may otherwise find nearly unapproachable. The men who want to be eaten want to be a part of us forever. It's about the woman either way...not the other way around."

"But why do you do it? I mean...why eat humans in the first place?" What she wanted to ask was, "Why did I cum while looking at my boyfriend's corpse," but she didn't yet have the nerve. "I'm just trying to understand myself," she said instead.

Tania smiled. "We do it because we're in love with the flesh, and when a man loves a woman so much that he wants to eat her, there's no better feeling of intimacy. We are so happy and satisfied to have a man who loves us this deeply—to be chosen by him. That's the dream, Erica. And that's the way these boys"—she waved back toward the men, young and old, hoping to give their lives up to untouchable goddesses for no personal recompense—"feel when one of us decides to give him a purpose."

Erica was confused. "What does it matter whether the fleshie likes it or not?"

"You've heard about sex slaves? Or forced prostitution?" Tania went on while Erica nodded slowly. "There's a difference between those people and the people who choose to go through the process. In fact, a lot of times, they don't even really know what's happening to them. It happens too fast and they don't take it seriously, because they haven't been taking it seriously if they've wound up here. If they're in this deep and they're not fully prepared to submit themselves, then they can't ever be expected to understand what's going on. The boys here are like that, and we can see it in their eyes. They have a lot of fantasies, but they don't ever expect those fantasies to manifest. When they start to toe that line, though, and then wind up right over it, their regret can cause them to act out. Skinsluts have been hurt before, in other clubs in other cities—but not here at Bazaar. We are very careful about choosing our fleshies. There's a lot of things to consider. But the ones we pick...the ones who love us..." Her voice dropped into a whisper. "The ones who choose to make themselves available for our pleasure are different, Erica. You'll see that someday."

How ignorant Erica was of what the boys were going through when they gave themselves up as victims! She thought again of her boyfriend's corpse, imagining him so clearly that she could see him on the table of their booth, his eyes staring lifelessly up. "How many of you...are there? Are you friends with a lot of the skinsluts here?"

Tania laughed. "We're all friends here. Skinsluts are friends with each other, I mean—and most of these aspiring fleshies already know each other. There's a sort of...anonymous connection. As I said before, we're more like a family than a community. We're a big family, though. We have many children in many cities, and Bazaar is only one of them."

Her eyes glinted with pride. She was enjoying talking about herself. And her friends. "Do you have a boyfriend, Erica?" When Erica shook her head, Tania explained, "The men who love us from outside the scene, the boyfriends and husbands who were part of our lives before we got embroiled and are permitted to remain—they are a select few, and best handled cautiously. Most of them aren't aware of this world. Some think it's a cult or something their wives do on the weekends. We want them to leave them alone, and they mind their own business."

Tania took a cigarette from a silver case in her coat pocket and lit it with her Zippo, then puffed smoke between her teeth as Erica interrogated on.

"But why did you come here in the first place?" she asked. "You don't look like a killer or a sadist."

Tania looked at her. "That's an interesting question. I think that's the real answer. I come here because I'm not a killer or a sadist...not illegally, anyway. Not superficially. I just have a private interest I've taken on as my livelihood...that's all. We all have our reasons, but we're all a little crazy anyway. If you ask me, it's not worth living without sin."

She exhaled a cloud of blue smoke and ashed the loose tip of her cigarette in one of the club's ashtrays. The imperiously familiar nature of the gesture at last clarified Tania's position as Bazaar's owner. "And that's why I like you so much, Erica. You see right through these things. Right to the heart of what's important. That's why you'll fit right in here."

"What does it mean to 'fit in' here?"

"It means you'll have your choice of many partners, and you'll do a lot of good for us here. A girl like you could convince a new fleshie every single night to sign a contract with us."

Blue smoke swirling from the corners of her mouth and clinging to her hair, Tania looked out over the crowd as she spoke. Erica looked with her. A group of men who appeared to be in their early twenties moved toward the bar from the dance floor, intent on ordering drinks and hors d'oeuvres. Erica could tell that Tania didn't like them—they were too young, too pretty, too obviously there as tourists to the skinslut scene.

"Are these skinsluts?" Erica asked, gesturing at the newcomers with her Coke.

"No way...can't you tell?" The older woman took a sip from her own glass before looking out into the room again. "They're just empty fleshbags. But, you know..."

Tania's eyes glittered like hard gems as she studied Erica again. "Maybe you can prove you're right for us. Feel like a little initiation ceremony?"

Erica swallowed hard. "Yeah," she said. She wasn't sure why she felt so nervous; this seemed like a natural part of getting initiated into any community—at least, she hoped it would be.

"Pick one of those hot little braindead idiots," she said, gesturing to the pick-up artist bros who, still at the bar, stood out like a sore thumb in the middle of the dark and depraved Bazaar. "Whichever one you think is hot."

"What? Oh, no—I couldn't," Erica protested. She was suddenly embarrassed, unable to perform on command, her resolve to be cool and mature flagging. "It's not my place to pick."

Tania laughed. "You have to! Go on. Take a good look at them. Which one of them makes your pussy wet?"

She looked over the six guys in question and finally chose a tall, broad-shouldered guy who looked to be the eldest of the four, maybe in his early thirties. He had an expensive haircut, expensive clothes, and expensively shined shoes that gleamed even in the dim lighting of the Bazaar. When Erica indicated him, Tania turned in her seat to examine the choice.

"He's not bad. You've got good taste, sweetheart. All right—how's this for your initiation? You go seduce Armani over there and lure him to the back room of the club." Tania jerked her cigarette at the red door adjacent to the stage, overseen by two bouncers and a camera. "And we'll take care of the rest while you observe how we do things, then join us for the fun."

Erica gulped again. After all, her attempted seduction of Brad hadn't gone very well. "You mean...I should just invite him to the back room? I've never seduced anybody before. Not really."

Tania's smile widened. "Ah, come on. I can tell you're a natural. Plus, look at him! He's got "politics" written all over him, and you're, what—16? Don't answer that." Tania held up her hand as Erica opened her mouth. "I just mean to say, I'm sure you'll be his type." She leaned in closer to Erica. "I've seen guys like him with my own eyes. I was your age once, too, believe it or not. You're right in that you don't seem quite *that* young, and it's been a while since I was a girl like you...but if memory serves, as long as you show him some interest with no strings attached, he'll follow you anywhere. Just give him a few minutes. All you have to do is take him to one of the booths in the back and get him to verbally consent to being eaten. We'll be recording everything."

"Okay," Erica said, feeling more than a little relieved by the idea of having to bait the hook for no longer than that. She took another swig of her drink and, having lost track of Armani, scanned the crowd of people. A moment later, she spotted the broad-shouldered skin tourist in his expensive clothes.

Her soda left behind, Erica lay her bait. As soon as Armani saw her watching him, alone near the main floor as if waiting for him to ask her to dance, he approached with a wolfish grin: sexy and evil.

"Did you come here alone? You know what this place is, right?"

She laughed politely, then leaned in to whisper to him while smiling. "Oh, yeah—I came here looking for you!"

He grinned again. His eyes were a deep, dark brown, which made him even sexier somehow.

"Well, you found me. And it looks like I've got myself a real pretty date for the evening." He reached out and gently brushed a knuckle down her cheek, causing her to suck in a breath. Tania had been right...leading this lamb to the slaughter would be too easy.

"That's sweet of you to say. I don't mind the idea of letting you spend time here with me. Maybe we can get a private room and have a nice dinner." She batted her lashes at him flirtatiously, trying not to laugh because in her head it all sounded so obviously fake.

In another intrusive move, Armani moved away a stray lock that had fallen over one side of her face.

"Maybe." He looked at her oddly. "Are you working?"

Erica blinked, much too green to parse the euphemism. Did he mean for the club? "Oh, uh—no, I just—" She tried to look around for Tania, but the crowd had filled in around them.

Armani gave a little shrug and fit his hand to her waist. The warm contact made her flinch in surprise as he said, "Then come on over and dance with me a while first, baby."

"Uh—" She hesitated a moment before deciding that dancing would be a good place to begin her seduction. If she couldn't handle that, after all, she might as well go home. The music was throbbing in the low light of the room, everything feeling somehow like a scene from one of her favorite porn movies. She took a few steps closer to Armani. Her heart raced when he looked back at her, a smile on his face. It made him look like such a gentleman—or what she imagined a gentleman to look like. His skin was dark, and he seemed very attractive...and maybe not quite as wealthy or refined as she had thought he might be when she looked at him up-close and noted the slightly secondhand quality of his tie. That encouraged Erica somehow: made it easier to conquer him.

It felt a little funny dancing with someone so much older than she, especially when he seemed more interested in flirting with her than in following her to what she claimed was a VIP lounge. She wondered if that meant she needed to up her game somehow. Maybe she should be a bit more aggressive...a little less innocent.

"How old are you?" Armani asked into her ear while she ground against his hips.

Erica flushed red. Was this really the appropriate moment to start talking about her age? "Uh...I'm twenty-seven. I don't know why you're asking..." She laughed nervously at her obvious lie.

Armani gave a chuckle that wasn't quite genuine. "You sound like such a sweet young thing. Are you sure you aren't a little younger than that?"

Erica felt herself growing hot again. She tried to keep dancing without stumbling. That was getting harder as she grew more nervous. Armani kept glancing down at her while they danced, and it made her uncomfortable to feel his gaze on her face. Was her age part of his hesitance? He certainly didn't seem to mind dancing with her, if so. Her face felt flushed, and she was afraid he would ditch her in his doubt. It must have shown on her face, though, because suddenly Armani leaned over towards her, his voice almost a whisper. "What do your parents think of you hanging around here?"

"They think I'm with friends," Erica blurted out. Dangerous to admit on many levels, she knew, but it built false trust.

Armani smiled and slid his hand along her back, his hand warm through the cloth of her dress. He pulled her close to him, as if to keep her from escaping before he finished questioning her. Erica wondered how long it would take him to realize that she wasn't going anywhere...but that he was.

"I guess it's fair to say you don't really sound like a kid." He spoke again, this time closer to her ear. She felt herself flushing a bit more as he spoke. Armani moved in front of her now and looked down on her with those dark, dark eyes. The club's neon lights were reflected in his pupils, and when they made eye contact, she could barely see his irises.

It was just like Erica had said to Tania moments before. Here Armani clearly thought he was the predator.

He had no idea.

Erica's heart thumped hard and loud as she asked, "Would a kid offer you some private time in the back rooms?"

His face lit up and his eyes grew wide as he leaned in closer to her. He took her hand and gently brought it up to his lips, squeezing the firm flesh. His other hand slid around her waist and drew her body close against his, and his erection pressed tightly up against her stomach through the fabric of his trousers. The sensation made her body pulse while he kissed her again, now upon her cheek, and whispered into her ear, "Yes...I'd love that."

His breath was warm on her neck as he inhaled her scent. Erica closed her eyes as his tongue slipped out and ran lightly over the top of her neck. Soon she'd taste him back. His blood, his guts. Maybe even his brain. What a nice idea! She giggled slightly and arched her spine toward him, then drew away to the back of the club.

"Wait for me, sweet thing!" Armani shouted. She barely heard him through the thumping music and surging adrenaline. She could only focus on what was going to happen soon. Her mouth had gone dry and her body was suddenly very hot. The bouncers guarding the door once pointed out by Tania seemed to recognize Erica. One punched in a code while the other stepped aside.

"It will be worth it," she promised as her victim caught up with her, "trust me."

Armani followed her through the heavy red door to the back room of Bazaar, then slid his arm around her waist and overtook her as though compelled to lead. At the direction of a female concierge who made smiling eye contact with Erica, Armani navigated down a hall lined with mirrors—mirrors, and doors to other rooms, or even other halls. Just how big was this place? It was all a little disorienting, and Erica worried she had no idea where she was going.

At last, a hot blonde woman with a knowing expression stepped out of a doorway a few feet ahead of them. "Are you two looking for a private room," she asked in a breathy voice, her eyes twinkling along with her wicked little smile. "This one's available. Please, help yourselves."

"The service here sure is great," said Armani in

a tone so oblivious that Erica realized he had to be drunker than she'd anticipated. Her confidence bolstered, she grinned and agreed, hardly even flinching when the door shut after them.

The room was designed for a very specific use, judging by all the leather and metal implements of more traditional fetish purposes displayed on the walls. In the center stood a dais with a low bed, its corner posts ornamented with dramatic shackles. Not a window was to be seen, and the only door out was the one shut behind them.

Erica had never been in a room like this before, but she'd heard about them, of course. She'd seen similar sets in photos printed in all the relevant magazines, or depictions in "find your fantasy" ads that cost thousands of dollars to respond to. When she was younger and more naïve, Erica had read up on it. There were some people who really got off on being tied up or whipped or whatever, but who didn't want things to escalate to the realm of true domination represented by cannibalism.

Maybe Armani was one of those people. She smiled to herself at the idea—that would really make it easy to trick him into serving as her first-ever fleshie.

"What's your name?" Armani asked. He frowned for a second, then fixed his gaze on her again. "Or did you tell me already?"

This drunk loser! Erica smiled, but inside, she burned with impatience. She had to get him on the bed. She had to lure him in.

"Why don't you let me tie you up?" she asked, ignoring his inebriated question and his sudden interest, possibly feigned, in her as a human with an identity. "You can let your mind wander while I do all the work."

Armani's eyes shone. He looked toward the dais and said, "You've done this before, I take it?"

"Oh, yes," she said, her smile even wider, "I'm a very good domme. You have no idea how hot it is to be controlled by a younger girl."

Armani's eyes drifted back to her face. He looked at her even more hungrily now. "I'm not usually into being dominated...but I'm open to new things." With urgency sparked by his consideration of her features, he bent and kissed her.

The heat returned to her face when she felt his lips, but she gasped as his tongue slid inside her mouth. Her teeth itched, but she controlled herself. If she bit down now, bit his whole tongue clean off and swallowed it, it wouldn't be half as sweet as what would happen when the skinsluts finally arrived. Besides...he had to consent, first.

Coaxing him with a curled finger, Erica drew back toward the bed. "Be a good boy," she told him, patting the mattress, "and you'll get a special treat."

A husky chuckle rolled from Armani's throat. He strode toward her with a kind of sexy swagger that almost made her regret his imminent death...but that very sexiness would make it all the more satisfying to consume him utterly. Her pussy tingling at the idea, Erica smiled as Armani draped himself across the mattress. Her eyes fixed on his, she bent and, one limb at a time, set about chaining him to the bed.

"This is very sexy," he commented in an oblivious way as she locked his ankles into the shackles.

Erica smiled at him and fastened his left wrist next. "Aren't you glad you like trying new things?"

"I sure am, baby," he said, his eyes still bright with anticipatory lust. "I had a feeling it would be fun to come here...I knew it couldn't be as crazy and fucked up as everybody said it was. Are you a skinslut, honey?"

Erica blinked. "Yes," she said, quickly, "I'm a skinslut." The answer, though not yet technically true, felt so right that it might as well have been wholly true. She smiled as she bent to kiss him, sucking on his tongue until she drew back. "And you must be into the idea of being eaten by one of us, if you're out clubbing in a place like this."

"Baby, I'll fantasize about anything once."

She made no effort to hide her grin, her eyes crinkling with mirth even as her heart raced. She knew that Tania and the other skinsluts were on their way. She only had a moment more to get Armani to verbally consent before the real fun began. "You and me, both." While her fingers ran along the buttons of his shirt and down to the obvious protrusion in his trousers, Erica bit her lip in a way she knew most men found immensely erotic. While she rubbed his cock through the fabric to make him sigh, she asked, "You want me to eat you, sexy?"

"Yeah, baby, yeah."

"Then say it," Erica commanded. "Beg for it. Beg me to kill you and cannibalize you...and maybe, if you do a very good job begging me, I'll let you feel my pussy before I kill you."

The drunk idiot grinned, ignorant to the looming end of his pathetic, exploitative life. "Oh, fuck yes, baby," he said, his voice hoarse with need. "You're so fucking hot...please, please, eat me. Kill me and eat me, baby. I'll let you do whatever you want to me as long as you promise to fuck me."

Erica grinned, feeling her pussy tingle as she heard him. She thought of the skinsluts and what they would do to him, and her cunt ached, her panties soaked through. "Very good," she said, stroking his cock one more time. "You'll be a perfect first fleshie for me, you fucking idiot."

The door behind them opened.

Armani looked around the room as the skinsluts

filed in, puzzled and mesmerized as these gorgeous women from the club, most of whom were scantily clad, arranged themselves along the walls of the chamber. Erica glowed with delight as they smiled at her in sisterly approval, already feeling welcome.

Less comfortable, Armani looked helplessly at Erica, then at the women all around. "Uh—this room is occupied," he told them. "Excuse me—"

Erica ran a nail down his neck. She laughed as she looked down at him, euphoric with anticipation. The door opened again and one of the skinsluts kissed Tania as she strode in. Merely the sight of the club owner electrified Erica's already aroused body.

"You two look good together." Tania smiled at Erica and her fleshie toy. "Isn't she lovely? So much potential in that little body." A few security personnel, all male, stepped in after the skinsluts and shut the door, then proceeded to blend into the scenery while Tania asked, "Shall we have a nice, sexy feast to celebrate our new girl?"

Erica pulled away from Armani and stood back to let Tania look at him, smiling in pride, a young lioness displaying her first gazelle. Armani, however, was growing gravely concerned. "Hey," he began, "is this some kind of exhibitionist thing? This is just, like, a game, right?"

Tania ignored him, focused on Erica. "Are you ready?"

"I'm ready for anything."

The older women smiled at each other. "Let's see what she's made of, girls."

Erica laughed.

All around, the light in the room changed, growing brighter as though to fully expose the sins that were about to occur. Music throbbed from hidden speakers and the skinsluts let it reverberate through their bodies, softly touching themselves and sometimes each other in slow, sensual motions. Fingers slid through fronds of thick hair and caressed ruby mouths. Bodies undulated, beautiful flesh of all colors and qualities flashing beneath fabric in cases there were any clothes to speak of. At Tania's gesture, Erica hurried forward to unbutton the fleshie's shirt. Armani's cock strained against his trousers and Erica tried not to show her immaturity by blushing when Tania unzipped him to take it out, but that quickly became impossible. Excitement electrified Erica's body while Tania gave the doomed man a handjob, her hand sliding up and down his cock.

"You know what I like about you, Erica—you're young, but you're driven. You're a girl who knows what she needs."

Even as he moaned, Armani's eyes flew rapidly among the skinsluts, with their gleaming knives, busts, and slowly revealed flesh. The stripped, themselves and one another, their dancing interspersed with lurid meetings of lip and tongue and body. Meanwhile, watching Armani's growing panic with erotic delight and feeling as though she were in a dream, Erica approached. Tania reached under her jacket and, from some pocket within it, handed Erica a small object that gleamed in the light. A knife, she realized in that same vaguely dreamlike way. Automated, as if the weight of the weapon in her hand triggered some inborn instinct over which she had no conscious control, Erica knelt on the edge of the bed beside Armani's chest. He watched as she held the tip of the double-edged knife between her lips for a moment, the two of them contemplating the fine point for different reasons. Then, as if she had been possessed by the object, Erica let her hand be guided along as the knife drew a glistening red line from the middle of his belly to the dark pubic hair denoting his crotch. He winced and shouted as the blade cut a wide but shallow gash—an experiment, really—into his body.

"What the fuck is wrong with you bitches," Armani cried in horror, squirming in his binds. "I thought that cannibal thing was just pretend!"

Erica laughed as her lips ran over the sharp steel, collecting the hot, coppery fluid of his blood with a moan the encouraging skinsluts echoed. With one hand still working Armani's cock, Tania caught Erica's chin and kissed her. Their flowing tongues mixed his blood with the saliva that ran between their lips, the skinsluts around all moaning in pleasure at the sight.

Then Tania drew back, and Erica was given the chance to focus on her initiation. Armani screamed in helpless agony as she cut into his flesh with the long, thin knife, slicing off a nipple and regarding it deliriously while he screamed and prayed. After a few long seconds and the realization that she had all the control, Erica put the little scrap of rosy flesh into her mouth. Nibbling it, she found it rubbery enough that soon she was forced to gnaw with avid bites in order to get it down. *It:* her very first taste of human meat.

"Hey, you fucking cunt, spit that out!" He cried in horror, hysterical tears running down his cheeks as his chest welled with more blood each time he heaved for breath. "Stop, stop! You crazy whore, stop! You're sick!"

"I know," Erica said with a smile. "I know I am."

Armani tried to break free, but the manacles held him tightly, and the knife was hot with his blood. Erica smiled as a few skinsluts hurried up to hold his thrashing limbs down, further limiting his range of movement. She went to work, scraping his skin off in long, pink strips. Soon Erica used her teeth to tear off pieces of his flesh, the skinsluts moaning with envy as she slowly ate him alive.

"I love you," Erica moaned as she took his cock in her mouth when Tania gave her space to do so. "I love you so much...the way you taste, I mean."

"You're fucking crazy," he screamed as Tania disarmed Erica to run the knife down his balls, cutting them free from his body at the second he unwillingly came. The skinsluts screamed in orgasmic satisfaction as his last-ever ropes of come covered Erica's face. With a wild laugh, her pulse rapid and hot, Erica wiped the emission away with her fingers and sucked them clean. Tania, meanwhile, pressed the knife against his throat.

"You can't be serious!" Armani screamed, twisting in his restraints. The threat to his life didn't even seem to register in light of his castration. "Please, fuck, you took my balls—somebody call the cops, call an ambulance, someone help me!"

Erica laughed as she laid her head back and slowly swallowed his cock. Now, when the flaccid sausage was sucked as far into her throat as she could get it, Erica sank her teeth sharply into his member and tore at it like a dog trying to yank the head off of a helpless rabbit. Armani's head thrashed against the mattress, his mouth opening and closing in a gag, a soundless scream, as though the pain were too great to be expressed in noise.

"What's wrong, baby?" Erica released her mouthful of bloody cock to tease him a little more. "Are you going to cry? I thought you liked trying new things...guess you're not man enough to be dominated by a younger girl, after all."

The skinsluts laughed at him as he regarded the ceiling in his inexpressible shock. With a dark chuckle and a glance down at Erica, Tania pushed the knife's blade until it popped into the muscles of Armani's neck. With a practiced jerk of her forearm, she slit his throat, letting the hot arterial blood gush from his wound as he thrashed and struggled against his bonds. His head turned away as the women held him down. Erica took her time sucking the wounds in his cock while the skinsluts laughed to see him try to scream through the blood filling his mouth. His eyes rolled in his head. With a vile strangling noise, the sound of a man choking to death on his own blood, Armani's cock hardened one last time: a death erection, Erica realized. She'd seen those in pictures before, but never in real life. Amazing that he could still get one without any testicles! It made her pussy so wet she couldn't help herself anymore. Free of all inhibition with the skinsluts around her cheering her on, Erica pushed her panties to the side and mounted Armani's cock in his final seconds of life. The bubble of blood rising from his mouth was enough to bring her to the cusp of orgasm, but going further seemed impossible. "It's so fucking thick," Erica complained with a helpless look at Tania, who laughed.

"Let me help you, honey," Tania said, taking her by the hips to force her down onto the dead man's big, stiff cock. Something tore inside Erica, or seemed to. She screamed a little, pain rocking her, then quickly giving way to pleasure that was echoed in the writhing bodies of the skinsluts all around. As the older women devolved into a wild orgy, Erica moaned to ride dead Armani's swollen dick.

"That's a good girl," Tania coached, stroking Erica's hair before reaching down to pull a long strip of flesh from the corpse. With a wickedly sensual little smile, Tania lowered the skin toward Erica's mouth. "Open wide, baby...eat your fill. You get first dibs, since you did such a good job killing him...I don't think I've ever seen a girl your age so eager to join us."

As the wet strip of flesh brushed her lips, Erica

moaned and opened her mouth. She bit into it with animalistic gusto, her pussy tightening and spasming around the dead flesh filling her snatch. "Fuck, this is so good," Erica screamed, her eyes practically rolling back in her head as she came from the rush of flesh and blood. "I'm so horny, I'm such a bad girl!"

"You're a very naughty girl," Tania agreed, handing her another piece of flesh to be quickly devoured.

"I am," Erica agreed. "I'm so bad. I must be—I love this so much."

Tania laughed and plucked up the forgotten knife, which she used to saw open Armani's torso with expert strength built by the dismemberment of countless such cadavers. Beneath the sheets of wet muscle and yellowish chunks of shimmering fat, Erica beheld a luridly fascinating collection of organs and entrails. To her untrained eye, they were nearly indistinguishable: a mass of meat, waiting to be used.

"Pick one," Tania said. "There's no rush. Take your time."

"Which one is his heart?" Erica asked, her eyes wild and wide.

"It's right up there," Tania said, gesturing toward his rib cage. "Jam your hand up under—just like that, good girl. Can you feel it?"

Erica moaned as, following Tania's instruction, she pushed her hand into the man's torso and through the offal of his organ meat, hot and packed so much tighter than Erica had somehow expected. Yet, as she pushed her fist up into the dead body, she instinctively identified the muscle of the heart at the very second she came into contact with it. It was dense, almost springy: she sank her fingers into it and pulled, astonished by the force it took before she finally felt a ventricle or some other vital strip of muscle snap apart. With a smile, Erica retrieved the organ and held it up to the light, admiring its dark red sheen. "How do I eat it?" she asked.

"It's best if you suck the blood out of it," Tania said, bending over to deftly cut out a piece of Armani's purplish liver. "That way, you can eat it without making such a mess."

Erica nodded and took a bite, sucking the rich, warm blood that rushed past her teeth. "Is it good?" Tania asked, licking her own fingers with a smile.

"Yes," Erica said. "It's wonderful. I love it so fucking much."

"Good," Tania said, smiling. "That's how I know you're one of us now."

Erica nodded, chewing and gnawing at the tough, thick flesh of the heart. It tasted better than any food her mother had ever made. While the women who'd helped weigh down Armani's arms helped themselves to the innards of the corpse, the skinsluts around the room continued to screw until the smell of blood and girl-cum suffused the room like an erotic incense.

As she ate, still rocking upon the dildo of the corpse's final erection, Erica's eyes drifted from woman to woman. The moment was one she wanted to remember forever. She absorbed every detail: Tania's expression of dark delight; the moans of the skinsluts in erotic rapture, exchanging meat through profane kisses. It was so intense and deliciously vile that, in spite of being trained for such things, the security personnel in the room were visibly uncomfortable— most of them.

One bouncer, a tall man with blond hair combed back from his brow, watched unflinchingly. Erica made eye contact with him for a few seconds: she swore the edges of his mouth lifted in a smile. Something about the intensity of his stare increased her excitement past the point of no return. Her hand, still around the fleshie's maimed heart, squeezed so hard with the rush of orgasm that the dead man's ventricles spat leftover blood in all directions. Erica moaned, her thighs quaking. Ecstatic, she raised a hand to smear the blood across her face and eyes as the little death erased who she had been before the night began. The bouncer's stare remained fixed to her, his dark eyes absorbing every second of her orgasm until Tania at last drew her attention away. Even then, his eyes penetrated her more deeply than the corpse's cock ever could have.

"Good girl, Erica," Tania said, helping her to her feet. "You're definitely one of us now...you belong to Bazaar."

"Yes," Erica said, wiping the blood off her face and licking her lips. "I do."

With a pleased look around the room, Tania put a stop to the wild festivities with a sharp whistle for attention. "Everyone," said Tania, "please welcome our newest skinslut: Wayward!"

The women whooped and cheered like hyenas. A few nearby patted Erica's head or slapped her on the back, calling her by her new name amid their congratulations.

And all the while, through the roaring adulation of the crowd, the dark eyes of the bouncer watched until the very second Tania led Erica away

When she was alone again in her childhood bedroom, Erica could think of nothing but the events of the wild night. The secret life into which she had been initiated had been so powerful, so overwhelming to her senses, that it seemed her old life should have evaporated. Yet, when the ritual was over and Wayward was given her place among the skinsluts, Tania had shown her to the showers and personally given her a ride home: somehow, the house of Erica's parents stood right where she'd left it.

"We meet formally on Saturdays," Tania had said, offering her a little card, "but you're welcome at the club anytime. Check the website if you need a lift back to Bazaar...we help each other out."

Now, in bed, Erica examined the business card Tania had given her. One side was labeled with the club's name; the other possessed the club's contact info and website. A different website than the one she'd found before, Erica noticed. Moreover, it was not the usual web address one expected for most businesses. This was a .onion web address, located on the deep web to bar normies from accidentally happening on the site and its controversial content. Luckily, Erica was used to consuming controversial content.

The new website, she discovered, was a message board. Intrigued, Erica scrolled through the threads to find posters with nicknames such as "Killer74," "Marauder" and "Chainsaw."

In the "General" sub-forum, there were twenty-nine current posts. Pinned to the top was a thread titled "What is your favorite method of killing?" (Knives were popular; baseball bats, though impractical, were deemed "highly therapeutic.") Another asked whether any other skinsluts enjoyed persuading normie boyfriends to join the scene as fleshies, leading to a long conversation between posters about various tactics of mental and emotional manipulation.

Erica also skimmed a discussion about what it meant to be a skinslut philosophically, though her eyes glazed over at the word "transubstantiation" and she quickly looked for more titillating reads. She learned there was a secret entrance for exiting the club if cops should ever show up. She learned they sold security footage to high-priced private bidders. Erica even learned a few helpful tips and tricks about corpse dismemberment.

Finally, there was a thread called "Wants/Needs." Here, posters were welcome to maintain a message with information on their cravings. Some of these posts made Erica laugh. *Wanted: Black or Latina BBW for luau fantasy. NO STDS!!!!* Or, even more hilariously, *Urgent! My electric carving knife died and payday's not for another week. Anybody in the city able to lend me one? I've still got half a hog hanging in my bathroom. Will share meat in exchange.*

And then, there was the one that truly changed Erica's life.

Looking to swap images with discreet skinsluts. If anyone has any interesting material fitting the below, please message me. You get unique pics unavailable anywhere else.

1) Photos of dead bodies, either posed or naturally where they were left (Edit: I mean photos of cadavers with decomposition and/or mutilation. Don't waste my time with morgue/mortuary photos unless they're mid-autopsy)

2) Severed heads/arms/general amputation

3) Mutilated genitalia, infected dicks, etc

4) Any pics of women being tortured and killed in graphic detail, including rape, dismemberment, necrophilia, bloodplay, etc

5) Pics of men being killed in graphic detail, same as above

6) Pics of couples having sex while or after being murdered, eg, dead cock stuffed in rotten cunt meat

7) Pictures of a woman having sex with a corpse

8) Fellatio with severed heads, masc or femme

If you have something not on the above list, contact me and we can talk.

AUTHENTIC (NON-CONSENTING) PICS PREFERRED**

Erica felt her pussy getting wet reading the post. The fingers of her free hand toyed along her clitoris while she considered the person's request. If this was the kind of stuff this person was asking for, what kinds of images were they offering? Erica's tongue darted across her lower lip. She did have those photos of Brad's dead body on her phone...but there was no way to know who this poster was. Their handle—"Kanniballer"—wasn't exactly revealing. It could have been some kind of cop for all she knew...but since it had taken her an hour of browsing before her account was approved, it also seemed likely that Tania, or whoever was running Bazaar's website, had vetted the identities of the individual posters to ensure they were actual skinsluts.

Besides...the idea of sending these images to Kanniballer appealed too intensely. The possible benefits outweighed the risks to Erica, for whom consequences were a mere fairy tale. Who knew what rewards might be in store for her? Her mother did always say it was important to put yourself out there and make new friends.

Thinking not just of her pictures of Brad but her father's old magazines from back when cannibal pornography was allowed to be hot, Erica clicked the username and began a message:

I can do #1 easily. I may also have scans of a few vintage non-con pics for you. If you're still looking, send me some ideas of what I can expect in return.

Before she could think about it too deeply, Erica sent the message off. She continued browsing the board, not expecting anything to come of it anytime soon.

Yet, to her surprise—just as she was about to log off for the night—the little envelope icon in the upper right-hand corner of the interface flashed bright red. Her heart leapt. She clicked on the icon to see Kanniballer's reply.

Hey Wayward—
We might be able to negotiate something that will be mutually beneficial. If you'd be so kind as to send me some ideas of the sorts of things you like, I'll let you know if I have images you might want to trade.

She read over the message twice. It was shocking this poster had gotten back to her at all, let alone so quickly.

"Mutually beneficial?" Why did Erica feel like that phrase had implications beyond the swapping of dirty photographs? Something about the message gave her pause. It seemed like a real point of no return: like, if she replied, she was consenting to something she didn't want to admit to herself. She had never done anything like this before, and that alone was enough to make her hesitate.

Sex and cannibalism in the private club was one thing. If she sent the images of Brad and left a digital footprint...well, it was a real risk. Cannibalism was legal everywhere; in most jurisdictions, so was consensual homicide. But murder sure wasn't. The idea of getting sent to prison at her age, right after she had just become a skinslut and opened a whole new world for herself—well, it was a bummer, to say the least. Yet...the temptation of seeing what this person had to trade was just too erotic to ignore. She wanted to add to her growing collection, mental and digital, of depraved imagery.

Her pulse pounding, Erica constructed a reply she hoped didn't sound too eager.

Thanks for getting back to me. As far as what I like to see in a corpse, my preferred pics are those that include graphic mutilation. My favorites include close-up shots of a human face after death (especially without the eyes or with damage to them) and necro stuff in general. Also interested in amputation and hanging/asphyxiation. You get the picture...text me at the following number if you're serious.

The excitement was too much. She was too aroused—yet also too afraid that the poster might not respond. She shut her computer down and went to bed, stroking her clit to thoughts of the initiation ceremony—and Brad's dead body, of course—until she fell asleep.

And it was like magic. The next day, she awoke to a text message.

This you, Wayward? I got a couple things you might like. Sent them to your account on the site. Confirm by sending your own and we'll keep talking.

When she opened her account for the images, she discovered another message from Kanniballer.

Let me know if you like these pics to start with. I have way more graphic stuff than this; I'm a bit of a gore whore. Tell me what you think. Are you into the whole skinslut lifestyle, or are you in it for the fantasy? It's okay if you're just into pic swapping, no pressure. Let me know what you're into, and maybe we could make some deals.

The images showed a dead man: one with his eyes blankly open while, affixed on a meat hook that must have been buried in the muscles of his back, he hung in a room filled with the bloody remnants of other dismembered corpses; and another, lying on his back in the midst of dismemberment, red meat gleaming from within the open cavity of his torso. It wasn't clear how he died.

If you don't respond in twenty-four hours, I won't bother you again—I'm not a spammer and I hate wasting my time. But I really do have some great pics for you.
Kanniballer

Amazing how just sharing these pictures was so much more fun than had been the mere idea of having sex with Brad...or with anyone. Without even getting out of bed, she hurried to reward Kanniballer's gesture of trust with her own original images: Brad's swollen face and lolling tongue and dead, staring eyes all used like traded baseball cards to indulge her pleasure with the tap of her smartphone. She couldn't get enough.

And neither could Kanniballer. He replied with another text message almost immediately—not with an image but with a link directing her to a private page where dozens of erotic corpse (or slightly pre-corpse) pictures could be viewed at leisure. Some of them were posed, some of them were in action. Most of them showed women, which Erica found extremely hot. They had all died gruesomely, but their bodies were often presented as if they'd died at an artist's disposal rather than an executioner's. Many of the bodies had obviously been arranged after death for their sexual presentation. One was even posed like a painting she remembered from art class: Manet's *Olympia*, re-envisioned as a corpse naked on the edge of a bed with a large knife buried in her throat and her lips sensually parted by her final breath. Another, this one of a man, lay in an almost comically large pool of blood on the floor of a bathroom, his parting erection clearly visible through his sweatpants.

Still others were more dynamic. In one picture, another man hung upside down from a hook and dangled in a dark room. (The room depicted before? Too shadowed to tell.) His face contorted in pain as a pair of female hands manipulated him sexually, pulling his dick like they were about to tear it off. It didn't take much imagination to hear his screams of agony...or pleasure. There was also a picture of a teenage boy tied upside-down in the middle of the woods, the branches of an old oak tree holding him aloft, his hands cuffed behind his back. Tears stained his cheeks and the blindfold across his eyes was crooked, allowing just a hint of the true terror and helplessness exhibited by his soul. The man who had captured the youth seemed about to castrate him: at least, a male hand with a knife reached from outside the frame, intent on the young man's genitals. His balls were already exposed, nested in the man's other hand, ready to be liberated any second. For some reason, that was Erica's favorite image of the bunch.

She knew she should be satisfied with these transgressions and go without replying, but it was just too good a chance to pass up. She couldn't resist getting to know this Kanniballer guy: not when he had access to such interesting pictures. Her pussy was wet as she typed a text message carefully constructed to portray a blasé sense of maturity. *Cool pics*, she wrote. *Did you take those yourself?*

Kanniballer's response was almost instantaneous.

Some friends took them. We trade pics like this all the time.

A little disappointing. She wasn't sure if she believed it. To test this, Erica replied, *Too bad! I was going to ask if you wanted help taking some more.*

She got another text immediately.

I don't take my own pictures, but I have a lot of cool stuff I can't share online. Are you local?

Erica bit her lip. It was Sunday morning. She should have been getting ready for church, like her sister and parents. Instead...instead, she was making plans.

I could hang out for a while tomorrow. Be at the bus stop on University and West by 3:30, Erica wrote back.

Sounds good.

Erica closed the messaging app and ground her tongue along her teeth. She swept through her phone to look at her pictures of Brad, his eyes open wide, his fat lips almost black with the excess of stagnant blood.

Amazing how much an accident can change the course of a person's life! What kind of future would she have? The question rotated endlessly through her mind as she stood to get dressed.

"Are you up, Erica," called her mother from the hallway. "We'll be late for church!"

Smiling to herself in the mirror on her closet door, Erica told her, "I'll be right there!"

Church! Church, after what she had done? It was just too hot. Erica groaned. Her pussy throbbed, sending a wave of wet heat through her body. Her clit was so hard it hurt. She wanted to fuck something—*anything.*

Erica slipped out of bed and into her shower. She was still aroused as she stepped beneath the spray of hot water. She closed her eyes and remembered the night before, the sounds and smells of the club. She'd killed a man last night, she reflected. She'd killed a man and eaten him. The memory of it sent another surge of arousal through her body. Armani's death hadn't been like Brad's. Brad was just an accident, really. A crime of passion. But Armani...Armani had been willful, sensual. Delicious. She was a murderer, she realized: and somehow, that made her feel *good.*

Erica stepped out of the shower and dressed quickly. She was still horny, and she needed to fuck something. Shuddering with a reflexive memory of the bouncer's stare, Erica grabbed her purse and hurried down the stairs.

While her mother helped her little sister get ready upstairs, her father was in the kitchen. He was standing at the stove, frying bacon, but turned at the sound of her footfall to offer her a smile. After more than fifty years of life he was still handsome, her father. He had gray hair and blue eyes, and a strong jaw. His body remained trim and muscular, and he had recently adopted a way of looking at her that made her feel like a woman. She used to wish he'd look at her that way when she was a little girl. She hadn't realized until walking into the kitchen, so utterly transformed, how much she appreciated that newly assessing gaze.

"Morning," he said.

"Morning," she said, averting her eyes and cutting toward the table.

"Breakfast?"

She nodded. "Yes, please."

"You want bacon?"

She nodded.

"Then sit down and I'll make you some."

She nodded, and hurried to the table. She sat and watched him as he worked. She still felt aroused, and for some reason—maybe because of the perversity of the secret contained within her—the sight of him made her feel even more so. He turned, the frying pan held high in his right hand, and smiled. "Everything all right, honey," he asked, his expression somehow odd. "I was expecting you to call for a ride home last night."

"I got a lift from a friend," Erica said—almost the truth. "Sorry, I should have told you I'd have it handled."

"Hey, baby, it's no problem…I just want to make sure my little girl is safe. It's a weird world out there… and that area of town your friends wanted to meet at isn't exactly the greatest. Even I get a little worried on that avenue. Ready for church?"

She nodded. "I'm ready." She smiled at him. "But first…breakfast! Don't let me distract you…you know I like my bacon nice and tender."

04

At 3:30 sharp the following afternoon, Erica met the poster at the designated spot a half mile from her college. There were no other students walking the road. Endless cars drove by, and every time, Erica's body tensed with anticipation. Was that him in that Jetta? What about that beat-up Audi? Was it Kanniballer driving? Erica wasn't even sure why she sensed the poster was a man—she just knew somehow.

And when his red convertible pulled up before the bus shelter, she discovered she was right.

"Hello, Wayward," he said, one hand resting casually on the wheel while his arm draped along the passenger's seat. His smile showed his perfectly white teeth, all the brighter in contrast with the sunglasses he quickly removed. It took her a few seconds to recognize him: then, she was back at the orgy, riding that corpse, her face smeared in blood and gore.

Back there with these intense black eyes and their overwhelming stare, piercing her the way they did now.

"Hey!" she responded with a laugh, running toward the car, leaning against the door. "I recognize you...are you—"

"Kyle," he told her, still smiling. "Shit...I thought your username was just a coincidence, but you really are the new kid."

Erica's nose wrinkled. "I'm not a kid, asshole," she told him while getting into the car before he could change his mind. "Kids don't have pictures of dead fucks on their phone."

"I did when I was a kid...but I've always been a little different. Buckle up..."

Kyle started the car and Erica sat back, feeling the seat mold around her. The car smelled like new leather and cheap cologne. She looked out the window at the buildings with their tree-lined sidewalks passing by. Even with the traffic, he drove a little fast, but she didn't feel unsafe. In fact, for as casually friendly as Kyle's conversation was, they'd might as well have been discussing her new career in sales, or her new hobby of Parcheesi. "So," he asked, "how's it feel being a skinslut?"

She shrugged. "Better than school, but still kind of shitty. Like, I mean, I thought about it all day, and being a murderer hasn't changed anything about me... just made me realize some things about myself, and the world, and whatever. What's your deal? You're not a skinslut, right?"

"Nah," said the bouncer with a shake of his head. "Skinsluts are women only...I just work for the club."

"But you must enjoy it if you're posting on their message board to ask for dirty corpse pics in your off-time."

He grinned. "You know what they say...do what you love, and you'll never work a day in your life."

That was probably good advice. Erica nodded before going on to ask, "How many people are cannibalized in Bazaar every year?"

The question surprised him. "What do you mean? Literally eaten *there*, or—"

"I don't know. Like, how many imminent or present corpses walk in through Bazaar's doors?"

Kyle shrugged. "Hell, I don't know. One, two guys a night? More on Saturdays. Sometimes a girl, maybe twice a month."

She frowned. "A girl?"

"Yeah, my favorite. It's rarer, though, like I said..." Something wistful was in his voice as he glanced in his side mirror before making a turn. "Most of the women who come to Bazaar are skinsluts, obviously."

Erica reflected on her conversation with Tania. "But skinsluts also want to be eaten, right?"

He laughed at that. "That's not always the case," he said with a smile. "But, yeah. Some of them want it."

The house where Kyle brought Erica to hang out was surprising. It was in a nice neighborhood, a very quiet area not at all unlike her own. He didn't hesitate to usher her into a deceptively suburban living room, where, in comparison to the sleek television mounted to the wall, the furniture looked secondhand. Erica dropped her backpack and enjoyed an abbreviated adrenaline rush at the sound of a lock clicking under

Kyle's hand. Behind the shut door, he looked her up and down and said, "Nice outfit. Catholic school chic."

That would be the last time she wore a checkered skirt. Erica gave him the finger while he laughed. "Just messing with you," he said while dropping his keys on a side table and sliding off his coat. "You want anything to drink? You like beer?"

Not really. She'd had about five sips of the rancid stuff in her life. But...the temptation to seem grown-up and cool was too hard to resist.

"Yeah," she agreed as she crossed the floor to take a seat in the corner of the couch. "A Bud Light or whatever. That'd be good."

He nodded before heading toward the kitchen, saying as he did, "You're in for a real treat, Erica."

"The pictures you have are that good, you mean?"

"Yes ma'am." After a little rattling in the fridge, Kyle came out with the beer—a Michelob Ultra, unfortunately—and said, "They're not just photos, though. They're videos."

Her eyes grew wide. "Oh God..."

"Shit," he said with a laugh. "Don't start praying now." He put the beer on a nearby table and sat beside her, then turned on the television screen. Kyle'd had the foresight to queue a video before he picked her up: immediately, the display revealed a short-haired girl dressed in a school uniform not dissimilar to her own outfit. The victim was at the feet of a man who, when Kyle hit 'Play,' bound her struggling wrists behind her back with ropes. As she fought and cried, the man brought a heavily shod foot down upon her spine in a brutal stomp that shocked her into stillness.

Erica gasped, her arousal—tacit but growing since recognizing Kyle—exponentially increased. "What's her name?"

"I don't know," Kyle answered. "He only calls her 'slave.'"

"How old is she?"

He shrugged. "Maybe seventeen or eighteen, I guess."

"Jesus Christ." Erica kept the cold beer bottle near her lips as she leaned against Kyle's chest. "Are there any girls like this around here?"

He grinned. "Just one," he told her with a quick look her way, then back to the screen. Her face scarlet with lust at once, Erica forced herself to nurse the grody beer and watched the video play.

How quickly her eyes lit with sadistic delight! It was one thing to trade still pictures. Another when you could enjoy the meat still writhing and screaming on the screen, as though it were still alive. Erica almost wished she were there aiding the torture.

In spite of Kyle's claims, the girl on the screen looked about sixteen years old at best, and her uniform had been torn open to reveal her breasts. The thick rope held her wrists behind her back, leaving her arms immobilized. After a little cursing and kicking, she was soon kneeling submissively before her captor, who now stood above her holding an electrical cord as an impromptu whip. The beating that followed was vicious, each snap of the doubled-up cord accompanied by a terrible scream even before the head with its little metal prongs came into use. Then, the rape started.

As Erica and Kyle watched, Kyle's cock was rock hard in anticipation. She reached down to rub it through his jeans, earning a brief glance and an aggressive kiss that was over before she could respond. On the screen, the scene shifted. A man entered the frame dressed in what seemed like a military uniform, or an outfit chosen to resemble one. He was holding a gun, which he used to fuck the victim's already bleeding cunt. After a few moments, he removed it, took aim, and fired into the young woman's chest. The visceral sobbing that had reached such an unbelievable height abruptly ended. That quickly, the girl was dead.

Kyle paused the video on a frame of the corpse, then turned to look at Erica. "Do you want to watch another?"

Erica shivered. "Yes," she said. Her mouth was dry with a mixture of sexual excitement and fear. "Fuck, yes, Kyle...show me more. Show me something worse."

"Want me to make it last?" Kyle asked, sliding his hand under her skirt.

"Uh-huh," Erica stuttered, her breathing ragged. "Yes...please."

He hit play. The video, apparently a compilation, cut to a different girl. This time it was a black woman, who wore a tight-fitting leather outfit with a long red scarf wound around her head to cover most of her face like some uncanny mask. Her hands were tied behind her back, too. A knife rested on the floor beside her, ready to be used against her if she attempted anything. As she was raped by the man bowing over her, Erica could hear him growling "cunt" at her repeatedly. For some strange and primitive reason beyond explanation, the gross muttering turned her on and made her even wetter as the poor woman got brutally defiled. It only took a few minutes of animalistic humping before he pulled out his dick and stuck it in her asshole, which made her scream and sob for her mother. Erica sort of wished the mother had been there...then it would have been even hotter.

When the aggressor came, he jerked the red bandana away. The camera zoomed in on the victim's exposed face. All of the terror and disgust that had been rising from her urgent cries just moments earlier was gone, replaced by a blank stare of pain. She lay there whimpering as the rapist wiped his cock with her face until he was clean. Erica had a feeling this was one of the same men as in the last video. Out came a similar gun: "Bang," it said. He tossed the gun aside and grabbed the dead girl by the shoulders. With one hard yank, he pulled her off the ground and threw her onto the bed. She landed with a dull thud, her limbs flopping loosely over each other, unable to regain any real stability. He then began to remove his own clothes, revealing tanned skin that had gone a little soft with age, but nothing above the chest that could identify him. When he got to his knees, Erica couldn't take her eyes off his cock: long, thick, and throbbing on the screen.

Sort of made her want Kyle's...almost. But it was much more fun teasing him through his jeans while they watched this fucked-up pig of a man violate the woman's corpse. Erica could almost picture herself winding up as a useless sex doll body like that. Then, she pictured how Kyle would fuck her defenseless dead pussy and leave her behind when he finished, if it were all part of some kind of kinky bondage play. The whole idea seemed exciting but a little disturbing at the same time. Erica felt her nipples get hard and her pussy get wet as she imagined herself tied up, fucked, and covered in cum while her body slowly began to rot. How long could a corpse be kept and used before it was just too impractical?

Then she looked back to Kyle. He was holding his cock, stroking it slowly to the images on the screen. As if sensing Erica's gaze, he turned to look right at her and grinned. His smile was so cute; Erica couldn't help but feel her own lips curve into one while she considered how unsuited that cute smile was to such a disturbing, depraved human being. While he was looking at her, she took his free hand and slid up her skirt.

By the time she was in Kyle's lap to ride his cock, the third scene played out in its slow, gruesome detail. This was the same killer as the last one, but in this third video, he used a knife. Because of the gag in the woman's mouth, there were no screams— just the sounds of cutting flesh and breaking bone to accompany the visuals of vivid red blood and whitish fat. Kyle groaned loudly as he fucked her, burying his face into her neck to muffle the sound. Erica uttered an animal moan in response, her body reacting to Kyle's thrusts and the sounds of murder. This was all so much better than Armani's dead dick! Maybe this was what she needed…not a man *upon* whom she could act out her violent fantasies, but a man *with* whom she could act out her violent fantasies.

Erica came just before the killer finished, which was damn good timing. They were interrupted by Kyle's phone vibrating in the pocket of his pants. "Shit!" Kyle pushed Erica over on the couch with a grimace to extricate his phone, his unfinished cock still straining. "It's the club," he muttered, rushing to raise his cellphone to his ear while, rising to his feet, he adjusted his jeans. "Yeah?" he said into the receiver. "What do you want? I'm busy! And anyway, it's—"

Whoever it was on the other end had a thing or two to say: Erica strained her ears to catch the gossip, turning down the sounds of murder on the television so as to better eavesdrop.

Kyle seemed frustrated to have been cut off mid-sentence, but he listened closely to whomever was on the other line. Despite her best efforts, Erica couldn't make out anything from where she was sitting. Not until Kyle said, "No...no idea, haven't seen her."

With a glance toward Erica that chilled her blood a few degrees too many for her liking, Kyle assured the person on the other end of the phone, "If I see her around, I'll let Tania know."

Kyle hung up, turning toward Erica with a new look of interest. "Cops are asking about you at the club...they want to know if anyone has seen you come by to inquire about us, or something like that. That guy in your pictures didn't happen to be named "Brad," did he?"

Her mind raced. "No," Erica lied in a stutter, looking back at Kyle. He grinned. "I don't think so," she revised, her cheeks growing warm.

Kyle sat down next to her and leaned back against

the couch, still stroking his cock. As Erica shifted closer to him, he caught her in another heavy kiss. The two started making out and groping each other until both were panting with lust, a small solace as Erica's heart fluttered with thoughts of dread. Kyle's hand slid along her knee, then up the inside of her thigh before moving under her skirt. He began to stroke her pussy again, his kisses more urgent by the second.

"You can tell me," Kyle finally muttered into her mouth at the sound of her low, long moan. "You killed that guy yourself, right? Did it get your pussy wet?"

"Yes!" Erica cried as she ground herself against his fingers. "Yes, fuck, it was so hot, Kyle…it was one of the hottest moments of my life—"

"Tell me more…"

Kyle pushed her down on the couch, kissing her passionately. "It gets better…" Erica whispered into his ear as he fucked her. "His brains were all over the fucking blacktop even before I strangled him to death, they looked like little cranberries…like a smashed jelly jar…oh, fuck yes, Kyle, you probably would have stuck this big, fat cock of yours through the split in his skull…"

"You love that, don't you, little girl?"

"Yes, fuck, I'm getting close again—give me another one! Fuck my pussy with that monster cock of yours until I explode, oh, Christ—" Kyle spanked Erica's ass while he fucked her, pumping her pussy with more intensity than before. Erica moaned as she submitted to her orgasm, letting her mouth run wild enough to trigger Kyle's own brutal orgasm deep inside her. "Oh, fuck…it would be so hot to kill somebody with you…"

The two perverse lovers lay together in the aftermath, Erica with a satisfied grin and Kyle with a smile that was gorgeous—and somehow sadistic. A wolf's smile, Erica found herself thinking. "That wasn't bad, baby," Kyle said with a chuckle as he pulled the Afghan blanket over the two of them. "Maybe you'd better stay with me while the cops are on your trail… you know I'm not going to rat you out, at least."

Erica sighed heavily. Something in her wanted to trust Kyle, even if she was a killer and knew the smell of one now. It was insane to believe he was truly fond of her, especially after only one afternoon of fucking to snuff films. Yet…the risk aroused her. Maybe it was the thought of that boy's death, unrestrained, uncontrolled by Bazaar like Armani's had been. How much she wanted to do it again, and purposefully! A true murder. If there had been any doubt in her mind, these videos proved to her that consent wasn't all it was cracked up to be when it came to snuff.

"All right," she said, her tone cautious despite the madness in her eyes. "Can you take me back to my place after dark? I need to sneak in and grab some clothes."

"Of course," Kyle smiled again and caressed Erica's face with his large, strong hand. "I'll make sure the coast is clear and wait for you while you get your stuff."

He kissed her cheek and got up, fixing his clothes. "You want a bite to eat, first, Wayward?" Kyle zipped up his jeans, enthusing with a glance at the disemboweled corpse still displayed on the television screen, "I'm famished."

05

One week later, Erica's mother appeared on national television with a tearful appeal to her daughter—or her daughter's abductor—to see the light of reason. "We just want Erica home," she wept, her face contorting with agony reflected by her remaining daughter, poor little Stacy. Behind them, Erica's father looked grimly on into the distance.

While they watched Erica's mother cry on-camera, Kyle had Erica bent over the arm of his couch to give her a good, rough pounding. Erica came within minutes, as always, and Kyle took his turn before she finished coming down from her climax. Good thing, too: his cock was hard enough that it might split the leather upholstery on his couch if he kept thrusting into Erica like this.

This time, he pulled out, leaving a messy cumshot on Erica's pale ass. He wiped his dick on her thigh before announcing, "Now you're going to have to clean yourself up before we go out."

Panting, a little shudder rolling through her body at the sight of herself, Erica twisted her head as the television cut back to the news reporter. "It's been over a week since Erica Cleveland's last known whereabouts have been accounted for. Anyone with information is encourage to call the Killborne County Sheriff's Department. Next up, after the break—"

"You never did explain why you're living at home instead of the dorms," he said while hitting the 'power' button on the remote.

As her friend turned the television off, Erica managed to ask, "Where are we going?"

"The bathroom," he said.

She stood up unsteadily, wobbling like a newborn calf trying its legs for the first time. Her dizziness—or his own shitty joke—made him grin as he reached out to steady her. Erica couldn't muster a similar affect, however.

"I mean after that, Kyle...you said we're going out?" Erica hadn't been out of Kyle's house the whole time she'd been dodging the cops. The thought made her uncharacteristically anxious.

"Sure are, baby," he said. "There's something I thought you might want to try. Trust me...it'll be fun."

Erica looked away and took a deep breath. Her pussy felt hot and swollen, aching from all the sex she'd had in the past week. Just about anything that could be done, they had done...or Kyle had done to her, at any rate. It was hot, but she was exhausted and a little freaked out about bumping into cops. They thought she was missing now, but if they had even a little of her browser history and still perceived her as a person of interest in Brad's death, they probably had a good idea that she was missing of her own volition—that was, on the run.

Still...

"All right," she said, limping off toward the bathroom. "Hold on...let me get dressed."

Ten minutes later, she was in the passenger's seat of Kyle's car while they cruised through the city. "So where are we going," she asked nervously.

"You're so new to the scene, I just thought I should show you a few things."

"Like what?" Still consumed by thoughts of the cops, she tried to get excited and focus on Kyle. Surely this was some liaison, and not a delivery to the sheriff's department. She was valuable to him, at least as a sex object. Her stomach was still fluttering with arousal from earlier—he had been so forceful last night...

But she wasn't prepared for what he said next.

"Theater," Kyle replied. As the light before them turned green, he put the car in gear. "We can see a show."

Erica couldn't help her scoff. Theater! What was this? He had to be kidding. Not after the way he'd fucked her last night—they watched a frat boy getting raped to death with a baseball bat the whole time Kyle sodomized her. Did he really expect her to sit through three hours of Shakespeare after that?

"Sure, baby," Kyle said, glancing over at her. She had to fight to keep herself from staring back at him too hard. "Bazaar does theater. They've got shows at least twice a week...I thought it might be interesting."

"They really do killing on-stage? Like, in the main club?" Erica ruminated on this, a little surprised given the way her initiation had occurred behind locked doors.

He smiled and put his hand on her leg, squeezing. It felt good. His fingers were cold, but the touch helped her relax a little bit. "Sure...as long as the fleshies clearly consent—I mean, sign a paper contract and not just make a verbal agreement—it's not illegal. No gray area about it. Come on, Wayward...don't be so shy about the idea. It's not like I don't know how much you like that kind of thing."

She felt herself blush, but she refused to avert her gaze when he glanced her way. There was something reptilian about Kyle's stare. She felt the need to meet it at full intensity and never look away. Only when he again fixed his eyes on the task of driving did she say, "I guess that could be pretty hot...do you go to this kind of thing a lot?"

He smiled broadly. "You mean, when I'm off work? No, no...I usually stay the hell away from Bazaar when I'm not working, but I thought this would be a good opportunity to...broaden your horizons, you might say. There's a lot for you to get used to, after all."

Kyle himself was often so deadpan that Erica was reticent to show any of her own emotion. Coolly looking on, she watched him out of the corner of her eye. "What are we going to see?"

"Just wait, baby," he said. He continued to occasionally squeeze her thigh as he drove, sending electric shocks through her nerves. "It's a whole new world you're a part of."

Erica tried to keep her hands from fidgeting. "I guess you're right. I don't even know what's out there—is it really better than the videos we've been watching?"

"This is different," he told her. "You've got to understand that...this is live. Or dead, anyway."

"Yeah, okay," Erica said. "I guess I've just never seen the value of performance art. But..." His hand on her thigh made her body so hot. Heart racing, she shrugged. "Sounds hot. I'll try anything once."

She only realized what she'd said as Kyle's grin flashed in her periphery.

"It gets me off when a woman uses that expression. It's like she knows what I want to do to her, and enjoys it...like it's okay to enjoy it."

"Most people don't agree it's okay to enjoy what we enjoy, Kyle...you've been working at Bazaar too long. You think it's all normal. If my folks had any idea what I was really doing!" Erica's head tipped back with a cruel, merry little laugh that seemed twice her age. "Oh, they'd flip their wigs...yeah, they'd freak out." She giggled again, delighted at the thought.

Kyle looked amused as well. "That reminds me, baby...if you're a cannibal, how else do you identify? I mean—do you like to eat men or women?"

Interesting question, now that he put it to her. "Both," Erica said after a pause, thinking about what she wanted him to know about her. "And sometimes

I like to think about eating both together." She looked sideways at him. "Like killing a couple, you know. Making a guy watch while his girlfriend is murdered and then feeding little parts of her to him against his will before he gets offed, too."

He smiled at that. "Sounds nasty." His hand stroked under her skirt, his bold fingers trailing over the damp cotton of her panties.

Erica laughed, letting him touch her where he wanted, her head rolling back against the headrest of the car. "It is nasty...it's fun for me to think about. What about you, Kyle? You work at Bazaar, you collect and fuck to all these snuff videos...do you ever think about really killing anybody?"

Kyle smiled at that while cruising into the lot behind Bazaar's glowing building. After he parked, he leaned in close to kiss her. When they got out, she him guide her from the car, holding onto his strong arm as they walked into the club. The lights were vibrant red and the atmosphere was electric, with people crowded in the shadowy bar area and filling the little tables around all the walls. Erica and Kyle made their way through the crowd until they noticed Tania behind the bar. She waved at them, motioning for them to come over.

"Kyle," Tania observed with a brisk glance at him, "I didn't realize you were working tonight."

"I'm not," Kyle said. "We're here for the show."

Unimpressed, Tania kept her stare level with Kyle's a few seconds more before jerking her head toward Erica. "We need to talk," she said, her tone harder than Erica would have liked.

"What about?"

Erica had tried to sound oblivious, but Tania's razor-thin smile was the expression of a woman who knew Erica better than she knew herself. Leaning against the bar, Tania folded her arms beneath her svelte breasts and said, "There are certain things that aren't good for the club or its reputation. I want to be sure you understand our rules here at Bazaar."

"The rules," Erica repeated.

Tania nodded slowly. "Yes, sweetie. There are certain rules I expect all the skinsluts to follow in order to maintain a proper and legal business relationship with my club. One of those is no non-consensual homicides." When Erica did not reply, Tania said, "I had the cops coming around here asking for you three different times this last week."

"Oh," Erica said, surprised at the revelation, flush with embarrassment to realize it had occurred more than once. They definitely had her browsing history... the devil knew what else. "Have they said what they wanted?"

"Of course not...but I do read the news. I'm starting to suspect they think you killed your boyfriend!" Tania raised her eyebrows, her expression serious. "You'd really better be careful, Erica. It's one thing when a fleshie signs on the contract that says we can do what we want with them. It's even okay in a situation like Armani's, where there's verbal consent—albeit more borderline. What's completely different is when you're killing some quarterback everybody loved."

"I—I know." Erica tried to defend herself. "But he—"

Tania held up a hand. "Don't tell me anything—I don't want to hear it. I hate lying to cops, and I already have to if they come around asking for you again." Erica exhaled slowly to realize Tania wasn't going to rat her out, then nodded with gratitude as the older woman said, "You're welcome to come here, of course, because you're one of us now, and Bazaar is a safe place for everyone who's part of our fucked-up little family. But you're visiting at your own peril. If you get yourself caught by hanging around here—if the cops come in and find you, or see you walk in while they're doing surveillance—we can't help you. Got it?"

Erica nodded. "Got it."

Looking not unsympathetic to the girl's embarrassment, Tania reached under the bar. "I know non-consensual homicide seems fun, but try not to make this a habit. Skinsluts get torn apart by the news at every opportunity...we don't need to end up blamed for your bad choices, Erica. Now, don't frown...let's get you some drinks and forget about it, for now..."

A little hard. Erica sighed sadly into her specially doctored rum and Coke while Kyle draped his arm behind her seat before the stage. She could smell his cologne; it was musky, smelling of sandalwood and leather. There was something comforting to it. Like the leather of his car: the smell of escape.

"Do you think I'm an asshole for not mentioning Brad when I signed up to be a skinslut?" Erica asked this while turning a pitiful look upon her friend.

"Not at all," Kyle said simply as he turned his drink around in his long fingers. "You didn't know the pigs would suspect you. Hell...most cops assume all dead bodies are consenting these days. They don't like the work. You're just unlucky, baby."

She glanced down at the drink in her hand, then looked back up at him with a smile. "I don't know," she said coyly. "I feel like I must be a little lucky to have met you, Kyle...at least, we have fun together..."

Kyle smiled down at her with his dimpled cheeks. "We do," he agreed easily. "We're going to get along great. What kind of drink did you order? Something fruity? Let me try..."

He held up the drink so he could sniff at the rim, then took a sip. Kyle let out a small groan of pleasant surprise at the taste. "Oh, shit," he said quietly, laughing to glance into the concoction again. "This tastes a little like blood!"

Erica giggled as he passed it back. "They don't serve food here, but there's no problem drinking it..."

"You're a pretty hardcore skinslut for a girl so young." Kyle laughed and offered her a sip of his beer, then used it to gesture toward the stage when she refused. "You ready to see what they do up there?"

Erica nodded with increasing eagerness. "If it's anything like your fucked up videos," she murmured, "I'm sure it's going to turn me on."

Kyle chuckled and put his arm around her waist, unnoticed in the packed audience surrounding them. "That's exactly why I brought you here tonight, Wayward," he whispered. His fingers trailed down her side and slipped under her shirt, resting on the soft flesh of her stomach. "I love knowing our tastes are compatible."

Before Erica could speak, the atmospheric music of the club came to a halt. While the lights dimmed, new, far louder music started playing, a deep beat thrumming through the crowded audience. Erica watched expectantly, leaning forward a little, her free hand falling upon Kyle's knee. Her attention was immediately captured when the first woman was dragged out screaming by a couple of skinsluts Erica recognized from her initiation ceremony.

"I changed my mind," the fleshie insisted, tears pouring down her face. "Help! Someone help me—"

Erica's breath hitched. On-stage, the brunette skinslut reached forward and grabbed the victim's hair. The fleshie's head was jerked around and forced face-down on the floor, where she moaned and wailed. One of the skins then began tearing away the victim's shirt, revealing her suntanned belly and a hot pair of soft-looking tits that the fleshie hastened to cover with her arms. Another skin took off the woman's panties and mockingly spanked her ass, as though it were an altogether simpler kind of fetish show. Erica shifted in her seat, turned on enough as it was.

The violence quickly escalated from mere public humiliation, though. One of the participants came up behind the victim and drew from her belt a gleaming knife with a cruelly curved blade. When the fleshie cried out in fear, the skinslut unhesitatingly stabbed her in the stomach. The knife was jerked free with a wet *pop* that sounded like a cock being yanked out of a wet cunt: then, it plunged in again, now through her soft flank, and the girl's shrieks rose against the music as her flailing arms were restrained by the other performers. Blood splattered across the floor.

"Oh my God," Erica whispered.

"That's not the part we came for," Kyle whispered back, his hand sliding down her stomach and beneath the waist of her skirt. "Just wait, baby...it'll get good soon..."

While the stabbing receded, one of the skinsluts yanked the fleshie upright to throw her into the arms of another performer. Two more girls grabbed the legs and arms of the screaming woman, pulling her limbs wide for the appreciation of the audience. While the fleshie howled in pain, the blonde skinslut took up the knife and stabbed her in the womb several times—the wounds were made so fast that the audience barely had time to gasp before the next girl came over, grabbed the blade with one hand while holding the fleshie's head back by the hair, and cut her throat open.

Erica groaned, sliding her hand higher into Kyle's lap. "You're right," she whispered, her hand fitting to the outline of the erection in his jeans, "this is fucking hot."

Amid a shower of blood, the fleshie collapsed. The skinsluts, bodies swaying to the music, gathered around the corpse, licking the girl's bloodied flesh, sucking her vital fluids from the gaping holes like a coven of spiders around the body of a fly. One of them turned the corpse onto its side and shoved its face into the bloody pool that had spread along the stage.

As she did, that same would-be corpse began gurgling and choking. Erica laughed. Still alive?

Incredible. Not for long, maybe; but it did make things a whole lot hotter when the victim was still aware of what was happening.

Kyle chuckled as he looked down at Erica's hand in his lap. She looked up at him through half-lidded eyes, biting her lip and squirming. When he bent his head to kiss her, she didn't hesitate to slide her palm back and forth along his hard cock. Her fingers slipped easily over his concealed dick as the fleshie moaned in her death throes.

As the women on the stage licked, molested, and gradually began mutilating the body, Kyle thrilled Erica by whispering his dark fantasies into her ear. "I wish it was you and me up there, Wayward," he whispered, "I wish they let men do these shows... oh baby, I'd love to cut off your cute little tits." Even as horror pulsed through her, so did arousal: Erica moaned, spurring him on to say as his hand slid down into her panties, "Would you like that? Or do you want to feel my teeth, instead?"

"Oh God, yes!" Erica leaned in for more of his mouth, his words stimulating her almost as much as the spectacle. She groaned, her pussy soaked, her need to get fucked increasing as Kyle's broad fingers slid back and forth along her clit in the middle of the public club. "Yes, oh, Kyle, I'd let you...as long as you promised to kill a lot of people with me, first, I'd let you do it..."

Kyle kissed her neck and whispered, "That sounds good. You're such a naughty girl...I can't wait to taste you, Wayward, baby." He pulled away from her and reached down to unzip his jeans. When his erection sprung free, Erica gasped and sat up straight again. "You want a piece of this?"

Erica was too horny to deny his teasing, but— "There's a fuck-ton of people around," she whispered, her eyes wide with embarrassment and excitement to see Kyle's twitching prick even below the table where they sat.

He smiled at her. "Don't worry about the crowd," he said huskily. "This is Bazaar, baby...you can do whatever you want." With that, he pushed her back into her seat and began kissing her neck, biting down hard enough to leave marks. Erica groaned, her body pulsing with pleasure at each contact of his teeth. She reached down, pushing the crotch of her panties aside before she felt for his cock.

"I can't wait to eat you, baby," Kyle purred in her ear as she began stroking him, each twitch of his thick erection in her hand enough to provoke a similar pulse in her pussy. "Ah...when I think about it, you have no idea how badly I want to fuck your tight little cunt with my fingers and tongue until you cum screaming on my face..."

Erica's breath grew rapid, her nipples swollen beneath the fabric of her preppie pink sweater. "Please, Kyle—do whatever you want with me once you've helped me torture somebody to death." She moaned, squeezing his thick shaft in her fist as she continued fondling him. One or two people glanced at them as she stroked his cock, but most of the attention was fixed on the stage. Erica barely noticed it anymore. "Oh"—she gasped, shocked by the intense pleasure of his granite-hard prick while his fingers pushed into her, pumping steadily in and out of her cunt with the pace of the handjob she gave him—"oh, yes, Kyle, fuck—let's kill a couple of people together, Kyle. I want to watch you rape a girl—"

"You'd like that, wouldn't you, baby?" Kyle said softly. "Me fucking another woman right in front of you... Oh fuck, I'd love to see you play with your pussy while she cried and screamed!" Kyle's other arm slid around her waist to pull her even closer to him. She shuddered and pressed her lips into his brow as he kissed her neck. Soon she was in his lap, her breasts crushed up against his chest, her legs wrapped around his thighs. "I know you want it too, Erica."

"Uh-huh," she whispered, tugging his prick while she looked into his face. "I want you to rape me...I don't think I'd even mind if you killed me...Kyle..."

He took hold of her chin and raised it so that they were looking directly into each other's eyes. "You're mine, Erica," he whispered, his voice dark and deep. "I'm going to have my way with you. I own your cunt—you can trust me to take care of you." His mouth closed on hers and their tongues entwined before he pulled her even tighter against him, his fingers kneading the flesh of her ass.

Somehow, Erica wasn't so sure he meant "take care of you" in the conventional sense...but then again, she was so turned on that she didn't really care.

The music changed. A new song began to play from the speakers as the lights came down around them, turning the club's atmosphere a little more intimate for the next act. The music intensified, but Erica didn't really hear it. All she could hear was the heavy pounding of her heart.

Amazing—she had never been so excited about anything in her life, and here she was, distracted. In all her teenage years, there was nothing she wanted more than to watch a real killing. The blood, the screaming. The idea had been divine...and the reality had sparked off a new sort of fantasy for her. Oh—she had recoiled when Tania suggested that Erica herself might like to be butchered and cannibalized one day...but, somehow, Kyle made Erica enjoy the idea of being chosen as someone's victim. She imagined the screams that she would make as her flesh was torn and eaten: how raw and pained her throat would be just with the exertion of her cries. Her nipples were hard and aching at the idea, her clit taut while she ground herself against Kyle's thigh. She moaned, desperate to have the cock in her hand inside of her. "Kyle..."

Once again, he flashed that evil grin. "I can't wait to fuck you, Wayward." He licked his lips, and she knew he must have smelled her arousal. "You're soaking already—just thinking about what's coming next, huh?"

"I know," she said in a low, soft voice. "Oh, fuck, Kyle! I need your dick in me...I want you to fuck me in half."

"Then maybe we'd better get out of here," Kyle told her, his stare intense with the kind of anticipation most often worn by a hungry panther in a nature documentary. "Drive around outside town a little. Clear your head."

Hoarsely, Erica nodded and dismounted before she allowed herself to be pulled along by the hand. She was in a kind of sexual daze so powerful that she was barely cognizant of navigating through the packed partiers of Bazaar. They went outside and climbed into Kyle's car, his eyes fixed on her the whole time. It was more than erotic, that stare: it was consuming.

As he drove out of town, Erica's heart raced. Soon after getting on a state highway they were driving off the main road and down a winding dirt lane that wound around a thicket of trees, then up again toward an old abandoned farmhouse. The trip had taken all of fifteen minutes, but Erica stared out the windshield like he'd driven to another planet as he brought the car to a stop in front of the dilapidated building.

"Are you sure this is where you want to go?" she asked, a tremor of fear in her voice. The sun had long-since set, but even through the gloom Erica could see how dilapidated the house really was. Despite his intentions to take her out of town, she had been expecting something more accommodating—some kind of hotel, perhaps. Kyle chuckled at her audible anxiety, his dark gaze turning upon her as he slid his fingers up beneath her thin skirt in pursuit of her clit.

"You'll like it, I promise." She gasped at his touch while he smirked. "I think we should take off these clothes first," he went on, speaking in a voice so low and sultry that it sent shivers through her body.

With a dizzy nod, keenly aware of how alone they were, Erica slid her sweater over her head. He wasn't going to kill her tonight, she was sure...she was sure.

Was she sure? Even as she kept telling herself she was sure, a little voice in her head made her realize how unsure she really was. Yet the heat that fear caused in her face and pussy was an irresistible blaze by the time, naked, Erica met Kyle's deliciously cold eyes again.

"Let's go," he said. And with his gentle push, she climbed out of the car.

She stood for a moment in the dark, looking around her and shivering as she wrapped her arms around her own waist. There was no other car, and no one else within sight. "You're trying to scare me," she said with a laugh, her voice barely keeping steady.

He pulled her toward him. As her breasts pressed against his hard chest, her nipples stiffened against the scratchy fabric of his shirt. His hands on her waist were as cool as the night air, but she felt feverish all over.

"I haven't even begun to scare you," Kyle assured her. His fingers slid down to her bare ass and squeezed tightly, causing her to jump. Laughing, he nodded at the old house, then released her to shove her in the direction of the porch. She walked behind him, unable to shake her uneasiness. When they finally reached the front door, Kyle opened it with a familiar jerk of the loose handle. It swung open with a slow slasher movie squeak, exposing them to the darkness within. Kyle held high a flashlight he'd grabbed from his glovebox, illuminating the deserted space. With a jerk of his chin, he told Erica, "That way," and, "watch your step," as he steered her into mounting the weakened old stairs.

Erica's courage flagged. Her voice caught in her throat as she said, "Real funny, Kyle." She looked back at Kyle and tried to laugh. "So where are you taking me, exactly?"

Kyle didn't answer. He led her down the hall, into a large bedroom—or what had once been a bedroom, anyway. There was a small dresser on the far side of the room. In the center of the room, however, a large black chair faced the only door. Kyle pointed to the chair, gesturing for Erica to sit. The room was empty otherwise, with a few floorboards loose or missing and stained old wallpaper drooping sadly as though to avert its face.

She sat gingerly in the chair, its ancient frame squeaking beneath her while she waited for him to explain.

"Now," he said, "the question is: Can I trust you, Erica?"

Given her position, the question barely made sense. "What?"

"Can I trust you to be a good girl for me? Can I trust you not to try to escape when we get into our real games?"

Erica exhaled, her hands tightening around the edge of the seat.

"I know you think you can scare me, Kyle...but you can't." Face flushed, she looked up into his eyes and insisted, "I'm just the same as you are. I'm not going to run away from this...from you. And, anyway..."

She swore she could feel her own pupils swollen with dark lust. "Where could I go that you wouldn't be able to find me?"

He kissed her again, more passionately than before. His tongue licked her lower lip, making her whimper.

"We're going to play a little game now," he told her.

From his jacket, he withdrew an envelope filled with photographs. "There are ten pictures in here, but I only took one. If you can guess the picture, we won't do it."

"Do what?"

"You won't have to find out if you don't fuck up." He held out the envelope. "Do you understand?"

Yeah...she understood this was a game designed to be lost. Erica took the envelope from him, then looked back up into his eyes. "Am I supposed to read your mind, or what?"

He chuckled, his grin broad and predatory. "I hope not...if you can, that wouldn't be very fun for me. I like the thought of you losing. But if you guess correctly, you'll get something you want. Do you agree to the rules? Or do you prefer to be left here alone, so you can walk back into town without clothes?"

Erica felt goosebumps rise on her arms. "I don't like being left alone in abandoned houses, especially without my clothes. Fine, psycho...I'll play your weird little telepathy game."

With a small hint of excitement for what she was about to see, Erica looked through the pictures. She wouldn't be surprised if whatever she picked was wrong...but it was worth trying, if only for her own pleasure—or her own lack of suffering.

Her hands shook as she flipped through the photos one-by-one, studying them. Her heart started to race, and her palms began to sweat. Her mouth went dry as she looked at each photograph, trying to discern which one would give away Kyle's intentions or betray his interest enough to seem like one he would have taken. To her surprise, the photos were all of young men, though it was hard to tell their ages with their faces often out of frame or obscured in some way. Their limbs were twisted and dismembered, their torsos torn open to expose violated organs. The one image that did show the victim's face revealed features mutilated beyond any repair, the viscera of an eyeball having burst and leaked across the victim's contorted cheek. The idea turned her on and she shifted in her seat, glancing up to meet Kyle's eye. "It'd be more fun if you were looking at these with me, instead of hovering over me."

"Just make your guess, Erica…quit stalling." Kyle said. He leaned against the wall in front of her, waiting for her selection. She assessed him as long as she could stand, her focus skipping over his underarm, waist: anywhere he might have a weapon secreted. Never in her life had her nakedness been weaponized against her so completely. Was this what the unwilling models in these photos had felt in their last moments? It might have made her feel empathy if it weren't so exciting. Unable to bear it anymore, she hurried through the rest of the images. Over and over, she rifled through them until she found herself staring at the last photograph almost without thinking about it.

It showed the most gruesome victim she'd seen so far in this batch…and it made her wonder what kinds of fucked up things Kyle planned to do to her if she guessed incorrectly. The victim was hanging in a basement room, inverted, his arms stretched past his head and nearly brushing the concrete floor. A woman in a blood-spattered bikini stood beside him holding an electric drill. The man's legs were pulled apart by chains that had been affixed to metal hooks stuck into the ceiling. He couldn't even squirm and was covered in blood, his eyes wide and horrified. All that remained of his genitals was a bloody mess, a gaping maw that looked black in the photograph.

And just as Kyle seemed to really be getting impatient, Erica recognized the woman. The blonde from the back of Bazaar.

The relief of victory surged through her and she sat up a little straighter.

"This one," she blurted without hesitation, waving it at him.

"Well...damn." Kyle seemed pleased despite his mock disappointment, although his smile didn't reach his eyes. "I'm impressed. I should have showed you one without a performer in it. Yeah, you're right. I took that photo myself a couple of years ago...back when I was a kid, just messing around. It wasn't my best work, but it shows what I can do. I thought about directing an actual snuff movie inspired by that picture once, actually...using a real victim instead of a wax dummy like the professional production companies use sometimes, of course...it's just so much hassle to distribute those things once they're filmed, and if it's for my private collection, well—then why make it a big deal?"

Erica's tongue darted across her lower lip. She knew it. She had known it from the second he first showed her those fucked up, sexy snuff videos back at his house that Kyle was more than a voyeur at the club where he worked. He had his own pastimes.

With a look around, she asked, "Is this where you take them?"

"You bet. That way, if they survive long enough, I can have some fun in a place where nobody can find them…"

He strode over to look closely at the photograph of the body. As he bent over her to do so, Kyle's hand fit to the nape of Erica's neck. She stiffened, her pulse racing with a combination of excitement and genuine, paralyzing fear.

"You're not planning on doing anything to me tonight," she said with a raw sort of laugh. An obviously false sort of laugh. "Right? Since I guessed, and all?"

Kyle's fingers gripped even tighter. "You'll find out in due time…but you've done well so far, little girl. Let's see if we can get you all worked up, shall we? I mean, it isn't every day that you see your first on-stage murder."

He pushed her hair aside and kissed her neck. Erica whimpered softly, but he didn't stop. Her heart was racing, her pussy soaked from watching the murder, and all the creeping fear he'd made her enjoy. The truth was she was already plenty worked up, and so intensely that as his hand slid down between her legs, she flinched. While Kyle chuckled, his fingertips found her pussy and rubbed at her slit. She moaned at the insidious creep of his fingertips along her labia and in between, clinging to his shoulders as he touched her. "Oh, fuck," she gasped, "Kyle—"

He chuckled against her throat, then lowered his attention to her breasts. He pulled at one of the nipples, tweaking it until she cried out and then biting into the other, drawing blood.

Erica was lost in rapture. Kyle's fingers continued to glide along her pussy, intensifying her wetness. The sting of his teeth made her tremble and moan; made her feel like a tender sheep in the jaws of a terrible wolf. He licked and nibbled and bit at her neck and chest, all the while stroking her clit. When he finally slid his finger into her cunt, she couldn't even think about screaming...she couldn't think of anything, in fact. She erupted in climax with an animal cry that shook the windows of the farmhouse. Her body contorted, arching away from him, her hips gyrating in a desperate attempt to get more pleasure.

Kyle pushed her down from the chair and into the dirty floor, where he grabbed her by the hips and lifted her up so he could fuck her properly. His cock looked ready to burst when he got it out of his pants. Erica felt so exposed, so vulnerable—she was still shaking, though not with fear anymore. She wrapped her legs around his waist as he penetrated her deeply, his grip firm on her ass. Erica screamed while he bit hard on her shoulder and pinched her nipples. The pain only made Erica beg, "Fuck, Kyle, oh, fuck—please, how many people have you killed?"

He laughed as he thrust into her harder than before. "You don't want to know the answer to that, baby."

The idea of him killing so many people made her want to cum again. A low groan of delight rolled from her chest, each hard hammer of his prick within her shocking her with another wave of Satanic pleasure.

"Kyle, Kyle, oh, fuck...let's kill somebody together, please—it would be so fun! Oh, I really mean it, Kyle, oh, Kyle...I want to kill somebody with you really soon..."

Kyle's hand slid along her thigh, keeping her splayed. "I'd love that too," he grunted, pounding into her with more energy than before. "I've been thinking about it all week, ever since I discovered what a fucked-up little whore you are." While she groaned at the epithet, Kyle showed his teeth in a cruel smile. "I think we should make our first kill a friend— somebody we know, at least...that way, we can all go home happy...kill them without too much struggle..."

Moaning, Erica nodded. "Oh, fuck, that's a good idea, Kyle. But...oh! Everybody thinks I'm missing...I don't think my friends would fall for that kind of a thing..."

"No problem," Kyle panted. "My friends are idiots—they won't suspect a thing if we pick one of them."

She nodded eagerly as his fingers found her clit again, increasing her pleasure and making her all the wetter while he worked himself in her hole. "Yes, yes! Oh, yes, Kyle...it would be so fun to strangle somebody to death with you...or to gut somebody together, oh, fuck, oh, yes...know any cute girls we could murder? I'd do a boy with you, too, though..."

She shuddered when he pulled his dick from her—she needed so badly to have him inside her cunt in that moment that she whimpered at the loss. Then Kyle grabbed her hips and turned her over, shoving her upper half up over the seat of the chair to give him better leverage. Like an animal, he mounted her from behind and kissed her neck with bruising pressure while he began to thrusting steadily into her. Her fingers sank into the worn leather of the chair; she braced herself against it, her cries of pleasure catching in her throat as he drove deeper into her than ever before. Each vicious stroke hammered his dick against her cervix, and the unbelievable pain of wincing cramps made her feel hot in her helplessness. Forget guns and knives and power drills: his entire body was a weapon, and she loved to be assailed by it.

"The problem," she gasped on as he slammed into her, "is all the girls you know are your age, Kyle—oh, oh, I want it to be somebody my age. Someone I could relate to."

Somebody she could fantasize about being while Kyle did the killing.

The answer rushed in all at once, plunging upon her with her painful orgasm. "Oh," she groaned, "oh, yes! Oh, fuck, that's it, Kyle, oh yes—what about my sister, Kyle? What about Stacy? Did you think my little sister was cute when you saw her crying on the news?"

Erica moaned loudly as she felt Kyle stiffen against her. The pleasure washed over her again and an immediate second orgasm began to build. Her legs trembled on either side of Kyle's thighs; her toes curled. "So that was your sister? That cute little bitch—I thought so." Kyle gasped out the words. "She looks really sweet...like she needs a cock in her mouth and a scalpel rammed up her ass."

"So we can do it together," Erica panted. "Let's

pick her up from school. She'll get right into your car if she sees me. Even if she gets scared, she won't have the guts to run away...yes, yes..." As the new orgasm approached its peak, her voice raised in a sharp cry. "Oh, fuck," gasped Erica, "oh, Kyle, yes, please! I want to see you murder my sister, oh, Hell—and after you're done we can butcher her up, we can cook her and eat her together!"

Kyle growled into Erica's ear, his thrusts increasing in intensity. "You're just full of good ideas tonight..."

He pushed deeper into her than ever before, feeling her pussy tighten around him as she came. Erica whimpered at his cock's relentless fucking; it was almost too much for her to take. Her vagina violently convulsed as she orgasmed, the pleasure flooding through her body like an inferno, the brutal cramping of her cervix afflicting her entire cunt and snatching hold of Kyle's orgasm without the least further effort. Groaning through his pleasure, Kyle continued to pound away into Erica's quaking, shuddering cunt until her orgasm finally began to subside. Erica shivered as she came down off her high. Spent, Kyle stopped moving inside her, coming to rest against her body with his arms crossed over her back. When the pleasure began to fade away, he slowly pulled out of her and let her slide down to sit on the floor next to him.

One might expect the glow of fantasy to have faded...but, in the look they exchanged, the sudden mutual understanding was undeniable. Maybe he really had been planning to kill Erica that night...but her idea had changed his mind.

"Want to do it tomorrow," she asked.

"Yeah...let's pick her up before you've been missing so long that she loses hope."

Erica chuckled. "That's a good point...all right. Tomorrow. Should we bring her back here?"

"I think I know the perfect place," he answered. He took her hand and kissed it, then drew her up by the arm and grinned. "How about we get your clothes back on and discuss it on the way home, huh, baby?"

The next day, Erica awoke from dreamless slumber to find herself thrumming with anticipation. She couldn't wait for that afternoon. Kyle had promised her a great time, and though she wasn't sure what to expect, she knew she'd be ready when it came—for some reason, she had a feeling he had been waiting for this day forever.

Her mind raced through the events of the prior evening. Would the plan come to actual fruition? Moreover, how would it wind up? She knew that she had fantasized about Kyle murdering her little sister before her very eyes while she watched. Yet...if she was going to do anything of the sort, she couldn't just stand there inert. Such a murder felt as though it should be meaningful to both of them, Erica and Stacy: a statement of Erica's absolute superiority, and the superiority of her world.

She could picture it already: the two of them in Kyle's car, Erica in the front seat and Stacy in the back, handcuffed to her seatbelt. She would be crying and begging to be saved—that made Erica instantly horny to think about—but she wouldn't give in, just like in one of those horror movies on late-night cable, or the snuff videos Kyle fucked her to. Her fingers trembled slightly as she thought about strangling the little bitch to death while Kyle fucked her...and all the things that would happen after.

When she heard a knock on her guest room door, Erica turned her head to see Kyle standing in the hall, his eyes red from sleep. He wore a plain white t-shirt and khaki pants and held a black duffel bag in his hands. He opened it and let her glance inside at the tools that rattled against one another in a mirror of her anticipation. The smell hit her hard in the face: sweat, dirty laundry, cigarettes—even the smell of human excrement. It was the odor of the world. How many places had this duffel bag been? How many homicides had it witnessed? She was excited and afraid and eager to wonder.

"I hope you weren't planning on sleeping in," Kyle said, his eyes fixed on her, watching every move she made in that peculiar, predatory way of his. "You should get up now. We have to figure out a little more about our approach."

She eyed the bag, nodding toward it. "What's in there?"

"Don't worry about it," he said. "Anyway...I've been thinking about it, and if we're going to use her meat, we'd better bring her back here to kill, don't you think? No sense in leaving evidence in two, three different places."

"Yeah, I guess you're right..." She felt herself becoming aroused by the anticipation, and it didn't help that he kept staring at her so blatantly, his eyes on her tits while she sat naked amid the covers of her unmade bed. "Okay...and if she tries to get out of the car once I've lured her in?"

He shrugged. "Can't you stop her if she does?"

She shook her head, laughing. "I doubt it. That little bitch has nothing but bravado when she gets into fights with me. I think you underestimate her."

Kyle chuckled, looking as amused as she'd ever seen him. He rifled through the contents of the duffel bag for a few seconds before taking out a pair of handcuffs, which he tossed on the bed next to her. "How's that—better safe than sorry."

While she picked them up, the chain of the cuffs rattled in her grip. The adrenaline had her hands shaking again, just like they had been all through last night. It felt as if her body was on fire with nervous energy. "Yeah...yes...we should probably go soon," she whispered. She looked over at the clock hanging on the wall, noting that it was already ten o'clock in the morning. "I need to eat something if I'm going to concentrate, and she's a senior, so her classes get out at one."

"Right, right..."

He walked to the dresser, where he grabbed a change of clothes and threw it to her. "Wear this so you don't stand out. Go on, get dressed. I'll be outside," he said. He left the room without another word, closing the door behind him with a careless slam that nonetheless rattled the house. Erica looked down at the clothing: simple and plain, nothing exciting. She slipped out of bed, dressed herself in the pants and t-shirt that Kyle had given her, and jammed the handcuffs into her back pocket.

Doing something else—going back on her word, calling the cops, contacting her parents—never crossed her mind.

A few hours later, Kyle pulled his car up to the curb at the end of a quiet street, where cars were parked along a few apartment buildings. Up the block, the school sat with the same nervous energy Erica felt buzzing through her body. All those kids, ready for the last bell to ring. Her sister, waiting for the last bell to ring.

Erica held her breath, watching in anticipation. Kyle reached over the seat and put his hand on her thigh, squeezing it lightly, drawing her gaze from the school she herself had graduated only last year. His eyes were sharp and focused. "Ready?"

"God, yes," she breathed.

He opened her door and got out. They stepped out onto the sidewalk together. Erica had to admit that it was strange; the air felt colder than usual for September. While Kyle hung back to watch her from the car, Erica made her way up to the school. Every step she took was a point at which she could have turned back...but why would she? What was the point, really, of having second thoughts? She'd eaten human flesh; she'd ridden a dead man's dick. She'd even killed Brad without any semblance of consent, though she hadn't really meant to.

Considering all that, what was the point of worrying about murdering her sister?

Erica was under a tree on the front lawn when the school bell rang. Early release students flooded out at once, oblivious to anything but the quickest route to the cars waiting to bear them home. So strange! They seemed out of a different world now: one she had vague memories of seeing, even being a part of. Already, it was all so foreign.

When Stacy at last stepped outside and, unprepared, set eyes on her missing sister, Erica realized with shock that even Stacy's face was somehow altered to her. Barely more than a week had passed, and they seemed hardly able to recognize one another. Nothing would ever be the same again, would it?

"Erica," gasped Stacy in disbelief, running through the surge of other students, unnoticed by them as they hurried on their journeys home. "Erica!"

Stacy ran over to her sister, wrapping her arms around her to squeeze her tight. She was crying now—quietly, Erica was glad to note—and clinging as if afraid Erica might evaporate. The older sister tried not to roll her eyes and instead patted Stacy gently on the back, saying, "There, there...it's all right..."

"Wh—where have you been?" Blubbering in shock as much as joy, Stacy leaned back to wipe her tears from her cheeks. "Everybody's been looking all over for you, Erica! We've been so worried—"

"I know..." They weren't far from the street, and the air smelled strongly of diesel from the school buses beginning to assemble for the students due at the end of the final forty-minute period. With a wrinkle of her nose toward the odor, Erica jerked her head back in Kyle's direction. "I'll explain everything. But first, let's get out of here—for starters, it stinks, and for another, well...let's just save it until my friend is driving us home."

Stacy frowned. "Who's your friend?"

"He's just some guy who helped me," Erica half-lied while she hastened away from the gaze of a curious-looking teacher, who seemed to me struggling to place Erica's face. "He called the cops and got me out of trouble."

With only a second of hesitation and a bite of her lip, Stacy hurried after her departing sister against all better judgment. "Did you see Mom and Dad already? What did they say?"

"Oh, sure," Erica continued lying breezily, luring her sister down the sidewalk. Seeing the women together, Kyle got back into the driver's side of the car and started the engine. "Sure, I saw them just this morning. Boy were they relieved! They must have really thought I was dead or something, huh..."

At the car, Erica jerked open the door and nodded her sister into the back seat. "Go on," she said, "we can sit together."

With only the briefest of hesitations, Stacy slid into the car.

Erica, who could hardly believe it had worked, settled in beside her and slammed the door shut a mere second before Kyle put the car into gear.

As soon as they drove out of the lot and turned down the street leading away from the school, Erica smiled at her sister. "This is my friend, Kyle. Kyle, this is my little sister, Stacy." Gesturing between the driver and her little sister, Erica began the process of weaving lie into truth. "Kyle's been giving me a place to stay while I was missing, Stacy."

"You've been staying with him?" Stacy frowned suspiciously.

Kyle grinned, already pleased with his new conquest.

Erica nodded at her sister's question. "I mean… yeah. I couldn't go home, and I needed a safe place to go, right?"

Stacy looked skeptical. "What do you mean you couldn't go home?" She glanced at Kyle for support, then shifted her eyes back to Erica. "If you were staying with someone, why didn't you call us? What would your mom and dad think if you were dead, huh?"

Kyle laughed as he turned onto the main street.

"They wouldn't care!" Erica snapped back, angry to be lectured by her little sister. "They've got you, don't they? And it wasn't like I ran away…it was more complicated than that. The police have been looking for me because of Brad's death, you know."

Stacy's frown deepened. "Yeah," she said, "I heard all about that. They even came to talk to Mom and Dad, and after a few minutes, Dad realized they were more interested in some dead boy you knew than in you. I figured they just must be confused. Have they talked to you yet?"

Kyle shook his head and grinned, answering on her behalf. "Not a word."

"Nope," agreed Erica, "not one! Very weird...but, I'm sure they'll straighten it all out with me later."

Stacy looked even more concerned. She pondered the window, then the handle of the locked door to her left. "So..." she said, turning her attention back to Erica, "how come you ran away even though you're innocent?"

"Oh, well...Brad killed himself right in front of me when I wouldn't fuck him, that loser fucking incel..."

Stacy's mouth fell open. Motivated by this reaction, Erica lied on, solemnly explaining, "I thought nobody would believe me, so I panicked. Kyle was nice enough to take care of me this last week."

"I can't believe it! Oh, Erica—how awful." Her sister shook her head, but she at once sounded less hostile than before, and even looked as if she might cry a little bit.

Erica smiled at her sister and squeezed her hand. "He's a very kind guy," she said, her heart dark with cruel laughter she somehow kept inside. "Really, just swell...and he's got great taste in movies."

This time it was Stacy who smiled at her sister: the first true smile Erica had seen on her little sister's face that day. Maybe the last one she would ever see. "I'm sure Mom and Dad are just happy you're coming home."

"Oh," said Erica quickly, a spontaneous streak of sadism darting through her, "I'm not coming home."

Stacy's face fell. "But you said—"

Kyle laughed as he turned the corner onto his street.

"Strictly speaking, Stacy, you're not going home, either...not now, and not ever." He slowed the car down. The house came into view, so benign, so simple with its dirty white siding, that it seemed as dead inside as a sepulcher.

"What?" cried out Stacy, while a sick thrill coursed through Erica at her sister's upset. "What are you talking about, Erica? What's happening?"

"You're staying here with me and Erica," announced Kyle. "And we've already got a plan for how to show you a really good time."

Erica felt like she could die right there and be happy, so full of wicked joy was she at the thought of the death of her innocent sister. And why? Stacy had never done anything to her. In fact, as siblings went, Stacy was practically an angel. She'd always looked up to Erica and shown her nothing but unconditional love.

And that was what made the idea of killing her so much more exciting.

Erica's smile spread wide across her face. As the car slowed, she leaned past the front seats and kissed Kyle deeply on the mouth. "How does it feel to have two girls living with you, baby?"

"Well...you know," said Kyle, smiling broadly as the garage door yawned open before them, "it feels kind of naughty...and kind of wonderful...like a whole new realm of potential."

From the back seat, Stacy emitted a little cry at the useless door handle. Erica laughed and turned to give her a cold slap across the head. "Did you think we wouldn't turn the child locks on, stupid? They only open from the outside...come on. There's no need to be freaked out...we'll have a good time..."

Erica gripped her sister by the bicep while she waited for Kyle to get the car door for them. When it opened, Stacy made a noise like a panicked bird. Her arms flailed, but Erica held her tight and shoved her into Kyle's arms before saying, "Don't let her scream so much, Kyle, somebody'll hear!"

Kyle chuckled as he picked up her sister and carried her, struggling, into the house. Stacy's eyes roved wildly down toward the big hand Kyle used to keep her mouth shut as he bore her along. "You're right, Erica...she's adorable. Especially when she's terrified."

Erica giggled and smacked him on the arm. "Did you think I would want to kill an ugly girl with you?" As Stacy made an awful shriek of comprehension that lowered off into a groan of horror against Kyle's hand, Erica went on with a playful coif of her own hair, "Besides, of course she's adorable...she's my sister, isn't she?"

"I like that you don't pretend to be humble," said Kyle, dropping Stacy unceremoniously upon his sofa. He turned around and grinned at Erica. "Sluts like you should know their worth, right, baby?"

He got her so hot when he called her that! Erica's face burned and she couldn't look at him straight, but he was smiling so broadly that her lowered gaze did nothing to diminish the pleasure: not when she could still see the glint of his teeth from the corner of her eye. In the doorway of the living room sat the black duffel bag, which Erica eyed while she removed the handcuffs from her pocket. Kyle kept a hand on Stacy's shoulder, watching through those sharp, wicked eyes.

Stacy looked up at her and made another awful shriek, this one of pain and betrayal as Erica cuffed her wrists behind her back. Stacy's face was flushed and red as Erica pulled open the bag, reached in, and took out what was becoming her favorite implement in film and life: the knife. The blade was a good seven inches long, its handle about twice that length, heavy steel with a razor-sharp point.

The girl made a smaller squawk of terror. She stared at the knife, eyes wide, mouth open, breathing heavily. Erica tried its edge along her thumb, wincing a little at the sting as her skin split open to yield a drop of blood. "Ouch," she said, sucking the coppery droplet from her thumb, "this thing's sharp...you'd better not move around too much, Stacy..."

"Why are you doing this," Stacy asked, tears flowing down her cheeks. "What's the matter with you? I'm your sister—how can you treat me this way?"

"Don't be silly," Erica said. "I wouldn't treat you this way if we weren't related by blood. Now..." Erica stood above Stacy to look her over with carnivorous appreciation, "...I think you have an ass that would be perfect for fucking. Don't you agree, Kyle?"

Stacy looked up at her, her terrified eyes pleading with Erica not to let this man rape her even as his hand slipped down to squeeze Stacy's rear. Erica laughed at Stacy's sad little cry of protest and brandished the knife at her. "Now be good and cooperative," said Erica, "and maybe we'll let you go home when we're through with you."

"Oh God—stop touching me, don't let him touch me, no—" Stacy wept as Kyle molested her, shaking her head violently. "Please, please don't let him hurt me, Erica! I'll be good, I swear I won't tell anyone about this. Please, just let me go!"

Erica smiled, reflecting on all the times she'd bullied her adorable younger sister for no good reason at all. Pulling her hair, hitting her when their parents weren't around, antagonizing her with mean names and evil lies until Stacy begged Erica to leave her alone... She loved it when Stacy pleaded with her. It always felt so good being a bitch to her own sister. There was something primitive about it: the dominance of one animal over a weaker one. Pure, unadulterated nature. Yes—it was Nature at work here. And there was nothing wrong with Nature, was there?

Kyle cupped Stacy's face in his free hand, forcing her to look into his eyes. "Your sister's lying to you," he said cruelly. "Nobody's going to let you go. First, I'm going to fuck your ass"—he smiled as Stacy's tears came in a new torrent—"and then eat you alive. But you know? You should be grateful to have this happen to you. It's a compliment. It means you're a pretty girl. Nobody wants to rape an ugly girl."

Erica laughed. Kyle's smile was very attractive, Erica thought, even when he was being such a bastard. Maybe even especially when he was being such a bastard.

Stacy was crying so hard she couldn't speak, so she shook her head rapidly from side to side. Erica looked at Kyle, smiling. "Don't worry, sweetie," she said. "Kyle's just trying to scare you a little. If you do as I say, and you cooperate, everything will be just fine. Just relax…it'll feel good if you relax. And if you don't relax, he might hurt you so much you'll bleed to death before we can have any fun with you."

While Stacy screamed, Kyle jerked her shorts down to her ankles. Erica raised the knife under Stacy's chin, using her free hand to keep the sobbing teen on the sofa. "Do you understand me?" Erica asked, holding the blade to Stacy's flesh.

Stacy nodded frantically, tears rolling down her face, eyes wide and begging for mercy. The rush of a good game rose up over Erica, who abruptly understood why the term was applied to the animals killed by hunters. Oh, yes…this was good game, wasn't it…

"Good girl," she whispered, leaning down and kissing the top of Stacy's head. "Just relax and enjoy this…you'll never have to hurt again once we're through here."

Stacy yelped as Kyle pulled his dick out and forced it in her mouth with a wet pop. She gagged and tried to pull herself off him, but he pressed her head back onto his cock with a hard shove that made Stacy retch. A streak of jealousy, of all things, rushed through Erica, who said even as her sister gagged and sobbed and tried to recoil, "Look at how thirsty she is for your dick, Kyle…boy, what a little whore! I'll bet you like that, though…"

Stacy gasped for breath, her head jerking away from Kyle's cock with each gasp of air. Tears streamed down her face, leaving long rivulets of snot on her cheeks and lips. The contortions of betrayal made her look very much like a pig being fucked by a human's dick. Kyle held her face in place as he continued fucking her mouth, grunting with pleasure and making her gag amid each deep thrust. Her tears and spit glistened on his cock as he came, semen shooting against the back of her once-virgin throat as her drooling mouth remained forced open. He was breathing heavy when he pulled his dick out of her mouth, his eyes half-closed as he enjoyed the afterglow.

Erica laughed as Stacy sobbed and tried to pull herself free of Kyle's hold on her. "You really are such a naughty girl, Stacy...how can suck my boyfriend's cock right in front of me? You sure do know how to be a spiteful little bitch, don't you?"

Stacy cried out as Erica trailed the knife down her soft neck, a thin red welt scratched along her skin. "I didn't mean to," stuttered Stacy, her face still gleaming with horror and sorrow. "Please, please, I'm sorry—"

"I don't think you're sorry enough," said Erica. "Say, Kyle...what's in that bag?"

Kyle looked up from tucking his dick away and shrugged. "I dunno," he grunted. "Some whips and power tools and stuff. Maybe you should go get it."

Erica stood up and fetched the bag. As she finally got a close look through its contents, her eyes glowed with sadistic glee. Oh, goodie! A cattle prod, nipple clamps, a power drill, some sort of electric saw she could use for cutting up flesh...yes, yes, yes! She was so very excited as she began unpacking her new toys. "Won't this be fun," she purred as she picked out the nipple clamps. "We can use these with the cattle prod...will you help Stacy out of her shirt, Kyle?"

Stacy's face twisted with revulsion as she looked

up at Kyle, her big, round eyes full of tears. "Please… not my boobs—"

"It's okay, baby," Kyle said. "Remember what Erica said? If you're a good girl, you get to go home." Taking up Erica's abandoned knife and earning a yelp from frightened Stacy, Kyle hooked the blade down the front of her shirt and tore it open. The handcuffed girl squirmed, pleading and sobbing while Erica returned with the small metal clamps.

"That's right," agreed Erica, snapping the first set of nasty jaws down on her sister's nipple. The sharp sting, followed by an unpleasant sensation of the clamp being tugged to ensure its security, made Stacy squirm even harder. She cried out again as Erica clamped the second one, squeezing this one extra-tight until Stacy was screaming and struggling to break free of Kyle's firm grip around her athletic body. "Would you stop being so fucking dramatic," Erica shouted, slapping her sister harshly over the back of the head. "You stupid little bitch, you're always crying. Well…"

Picking up the cattle prod with a laugh, Erica said, "I'll give you something to cry about."

Kyle smiled wickedly at his partner's enthusiasm, and Erica smiled back. It was so nice to be understood. Erica knew Kyle loved watching this because she knew he could tell what was going through her head when she tortured a girl—what her mind would be picturing, fantasizing, wishing for, and wanting. Erica's flush face and heavy breathing told only part of the story. She knew Kyle could see the rest in her eyes—in her eager hand as she shoved the prod into her sister's bare stomach and shocked Stacy with a crack of electrical agony. "Fuck yeah," Kyle moaned. When the shock had passed, he once more grabbed Stacy's hips to keep her in place while she struggled wildly to get away from the shocking prong. The high schooler shrieked with terror as the pain grew, but there was no way she was going anywhere. When the prod was applied to her clamped nipple and the conductive metal burned her skin with the sudden aroma of cooking meat, her sobs became so wild and sharp they could not be heard at all. Stacy choked on her tears, her chest heaving, her eyes wild with pain and confusion.

"Oh my god...that stinks!" gasped Erica when she realized that she herself was smelling cooking meat, too.

Kyle laughed. "It's the burning hair...don't worry. When we've bled and butchered her and cooked her properly, she'll just smell like cooking pork...even now, I don't know, it doesn't smell too bad to me. More like hot dogs than anything else."

Erica drew back the cattle prod, lowering the hot tip for a few seconds. Stacy panted for air, trying to control herself. She wanted to scream again, but it was as though the pain prevented her from doing so. They most she could do was make a few futile efforts to rise. Her body writhed as she squirmed against Kyle, desperate to break free. He held her so tightly every attempt to escape seemed worthless. Her mind flew with countless questions, all of them visible in her terrorized face. Would she ever see her parents again? Had she eaten her last meal without knowing? Was she going to die?

Erica sneered at her sister. "Penny for your thoughts?"

"Why," gasped Stacy. "Why are you being so mean?"

What a child! Erica rolled her eyes and insisted, "You could never understand...you can't understand, you'll never be able to. When I killed Brad"—Stacy gasped at Erica's admission while the cattle prod anticipatorily crackled in the background—"I learned something real about myself. When it comes to the sorts of shit I like, it isn't enough just watching, or fantasizing. I like *doing*, Stacy. I need *experiences*. And if you really want the truth, all my favorite experiences are sick, sick ones."

"But," said Stacy, "why am I just a victim to you? Don't I matter at all?"

Erica's eyes were dark with malice. She had been thinking about this sort of thing a lot lately, but especially after initiating into the skinsluts and hooking up with Kyle. It was all those videos. They required a certain level of justification...and justification required a level of philosophical thinking at which she'd sneered while browsing the website for Bazaar.

"Sure," Erica said, "you matter...think of all the pleasure you're bringing us! Think of how nice of you it is to let us eat your tasty girlmeat when you're dead. In fact...since you'll be dying here, you might even say that's the only reason you were born."

Stacy wept quietly on the couch. With a gay little laugh, Erica turned to smile at Kyle. "Do you want to go get that rope from the bag? We can finish the job before she gets any louder."

"Good idea," said Kyle. "I'd rather kill her quickly. Torture is fun, but it's kind of repetitive after a while. That's not to say that the next part won't hurt…"

While Kyle stalked off for the duffel bag, Erica watched him with a crooked grin. Ah! He was sexy. An asshole, but sexy. Not that she wasn't an asshole, of course…by any definition, Erica was discovering that to be the case. But how could she help the way the world chose to view people like her? After all, like she thought only earlier—all she did was pursue her own nature. And it seemed so much more honest and natural to act as nature wanted than to feel guilty about pursuing her inclinations.

Movement drew her attention to the left. She turned just in time to see Stacy with the knife that Kyle had dropped in the couch beside her. Her hands were still bound behind her back, but with a sharp thrashing of her lithe body, Stacy somehow managed to haphazardly slash the blade across Erica's forearms. As Erica cried out and dropped the cattle prod, Stacy, still bound, sprang up to sprint through the house with a window-rattling scream.

Kyle missed a chance to grab the girl, who darted just past him toward the foyer. He and Erica followed, with Erica shouting after the fleeing girl, "Stacy, wait!"

But she was no fool. Her chest rising and falling with the rapid breath of exertion, Stacy sprinted to the front door and twisted at the waist to try the locked knob. Frustrated by her attempts to unlock it—and able to make eye contact with her captors as they closed in—she abandoned that effort and dashed up the stairs. Tears still streamed down her face, but she no longer wept. She only ran, ran and prayed, and turned the corner of the second floor to find her prayers were answered.

At the corridor's end stood a window overlooking the front yard.

"Stacy," called Erica as Kyle sprinted up the stairs, "come on, relax! It was just a little joke!"

Certain her choice was between a death forever unsolved and a death that was at least understood, Stacy lowered her head, rushed down the hall, and threw herself through the glass of the shut window with her eyes squeezed shut.

Erica gasped. Kyle cursed and lunged for the girl as she tumbled through the pane, but he caught only air.

With a hard crack and a heavy thump, Stacy landed on the asphalt driveway below. Her body lay crumpled amid a heap of broken glass, as unnaturally twisted from a bad landing as the limbs of a mannequin flung accidentally from the bed of a delivery truck.

"Fuck," whispered Erica, panic rising in her not for her sister's death but for the inevitability of discovery. "Fuck! Oh, fuck, Kyle—"

"It's okay, it's okay!" Kyle ran down the stairs, his hands shaking as Erica hurried after him. Together, they ran outside to see if the situation was salvageable.

Stacy lay silent, her face pressed into the blacktop. Blood trickled down her temple, pooling around her to seep as far as the edge of grass beyond. Half-naked, bloody, cut to ribbons by the glass through which she'd propelled herself, Stacy lay in a tableau of meaningless disaster. An entire life, ended. Wasted.

"She should have let us eat her," said Erica with contempt as Kyle shut the door. "Would have been better...what the hell do we do now?"

Kyle shook his head. "I guess we should just get going...maybe we should have gone with the farmhouse after all. Why the hell did you let me take her here, anyway?" Before Erica could even articulate her scoff of disgust to realize he was blaming her for his shitty idea, he went on, "We can stay there until the heat is off, at least...if it ever comes off for you."

Erica nodded and turned to hurry back upstairs for whatever clothes she could grab in two minutes. Before she could step away, Kyle grabbed her shoulder in that viselike grip of his. His gaze was hard as stone.

"What the fuck happened back there, Erica?"

"You're the one who left the knife right by her," Erica protested tersely, jerking out of Kyle's grip and rushing up the stairs. "Don't act like I'm the only idiot here today...especially not when there'll be plenty of time to discuss it later."

07

Erica stared at the ceiling of the rotting farmhouse. The springs of the thin mattress jutted up into her back while, somewhere, something dripped despite the lack of running water.

When Kyle filled the doorway, she sat up before he could nudge her with his boot. "I got my last paycheck from Bazaar," he said, tossing a wrinkled brown fast-food bag into her lap. "You can have the rest of that."

Erica hastily opened the bag and stuffed her face with lukewarm fries that, after a week of intermittent meals stolen from the breakfast buffet of a nearby Holiday Inn Express, tasted better than any fresh one's she'd ever had. "I don't see why you had to quit Bazaar," she said in annoyance. "Surely they could cover for you."

"It's too close to home, baby, and I mean that literally...anyway, you heard what Tania said about cops. No..." Kyle contemplated Erica very carefully while she licked flecks of greasy salt from her fingers. "I'm gonna have to move out of town altogether once things have cooled down more."

That stare of his. Erica casually averted her eyes and pulled a half-eaten burger out of the bag. "Great. You can just kill me and be on your way." She tried to sound sarcastic rather than afraid, but the idea had surely been on his mind as much as it had been on hers for the past few days.

"Yeah...I could." In that empty, somehow malicious way of his, he smiled slightly. Erica gave him a sharp sidelong look.

"Just so you know, Kyle, I was kidding. Really, though, what the hell—*I'm* gonna have to move out of town." Do you mean you're not going to take me with you?"

He shrugged. "What am I supposed to do? I mean, anybody who sees us together is going to recognize us from the news."

Erica ground her teeth. Yeah, it was true. She didn't have a phone and couldn't watch TV outside of the precious minutes they spent stealing cereal and soggy old melon balls, but she knew from the little battery-powered radio they used sometimes that the teacher at Stacy's school had provided some kind of information to police. The news never specified what the information was, but Erica and Kyle both had a good idea.

"Still," Erica protested, "you can't just leave me here!"

Kyle stared down at her, then looked back up at the ceiling. A long, heavy silence followed before he said, "You know, we could make some extra money."

Erica frowned suspiciously. "How would we do that?"

"Well, if you want, we could do some freelance killings. Maybe get into kidnapping or something." There was an odd gleam in his eyes. "You know... murder for hire."

Famished though she was, she paused in her eating to process the thought. "Damn," she said, "that's a good idea! That's a really good fucking idea, Kyle." Her sharp eyes raised to his. "It can't be that easy though, right?"

Kyle shrugged. "I know some people I could talk to. It might work out great in the end."

"You know," she replied slowly, grinning a little around her next bite of burger, "we make a pretty good team, Kyle."

Kyle grinned at her and bent down to lick a small bite of food off his lower lip. "We sure do. We could start a little business together—just us. We could split whatever we earn right down the middle." He smiled again, perhaps at his phrasing. "Then, when we each have some cash, we can decide how to proceed."

He looked down at her, a hungry glint in his eye. "I don't want you getting the wrong idea, though," he added, God only knew what black and hideous thoughts rotating through his mind as he studied the girl. "This has to remain under the table, very subtle, since we're talking about non-consensual homicides... if and when I bring you to meet the guy I'm thinking of, you'll have to be discreet."

Now...Erica wasn't stupid. She felt the intensity of Kyle's stare; the dark anticipation in them. She knew there was something there. Something ugly. A new evil lurking behind his words: new, because this was the first time his evil had been clearly, consciously directed at her.

But...she was also a captive, in effect. Yes—captive to him and his will and whatever he wanted to do with her, until the very moment she snapped and handed herself over to the cops.

And Erica just couldn't imagine a world where she was ever willing to do that.

"This guy you're talking about," said Erica casually, sucking ketchup from her fingers before wiping her hands on the wax paper the eaten burger had arrived in, "is this the guy you get your snuff videos from?"

"Yeah," he replied, lowering down into the mattress beside her with a lazy half-smile. "He's got connections. I figure we can arrange something with him."

"I'm suddenly not sure if you know what 'snuff' means," said Erica carefully, her gaze flickering to the window and the darkened sky beyond before returning to the man who'd brought her to stay here in the first place. "It's a type of video where attractive young people—especially young women—get killed, remember? What I mean to say is, my role isn't usually the one doing the killing in those videos."

Kyle's gaze never flagged. It was like trying to out-stare a statue. "I understand what 'snuff' means, smartass, and I don't want that for you...that's not why I suggested you come along to meet him with me.

But I do think there might be an opportunity for us to make some extra money. It's something I've been looking into for a while, actually."

Erica wasn't buying it. It seemed like a lie designed to get her to come along to her death without a fuss. "I don't think most criminal connections are going to be comfortable with hiring a hitwoman who's not even twenty years old yet."

Kyle shook his head and chuckled softly, the sound of it low and dark and sensual even now—maybe moreso than ever before, her predilections having crossed the wires of survival with the wires of sex. "Maybe not, but you'll have a better shot if I vouch for you. I'm not talking about mob hits, or anything too organized; just the possibility of making some cash from our little hobby." His gaze dropped to her lips. "We could go into this business together. If you're willing...if you'd like that..."

"I don't know," said Erica. "It feels like you're leading me down a path to something...bad. Something I can't turn away from."

His hand drifted to her throat. He traced the soft skin of her collarbone with his fingers and let his thumb press into the back of her neck, his entire hand ready to become a restraint at any time. "There's no turning away, baby. That's not how it works for us. You already went down that road...the only way of getting out is going farther on."

Erica stared at him for several seconds, wondering how she was supposed to feel about such things. She thought of her sister and how she'd died, murdered in such a public way. Of Brad, a pure accident that she'd exploited for her own enjoyment. Of restrained Armani dying in the back of Bazaar, wheezing out his last breath while she rode his cock. Yes: Armani again, the other girls still around, giggling at the spectacle, all but eating popcorn to watch him die. Those women had supported each other. For a fleeting moment, Erica had been a skinslut just like them. She was still, surely—no matter what she had done or not done, said or not said.

"Maybe if I went back to Bazaar," said Erica, talking quickly as Kyle slid his hand down her arm and around her wrist as though to hold her hand, "they could help me—us. Maybe they could get us out of town."

Kyle smiled: a smile so gentle that it seemed like a mask for something else. He kissed her on the lips, sliding his hand up under her sweater and into her bra, massaging her breast with firm fingers. Erica moaned and pressed closer, wrapping her arms around Kyle's shoulders and kissing him back passionately, pushing her tongue into his mouth. Her eyes, meanwhile, scanned rapidly around the room. He was smarter than to leave her with access to anything resembling a weapon: he had been from the start. All the tools he'd shown her to scare her the last time the first time they were at this place had been taken away. But...if he had designs to traffic her to this snuff dealer, then Kyle might have had a weapon already on him. Erica's free hand slid down his back, intent on his jeans. He caught her elbow, freezing her arm in place.

"I'm going to kill you if you try that," he said quietly. "And I don't want to be in any hurry about it."

Erica felt a flash of annoyance amid the panic.

Clenching her teeth, her eyes blazing, she told him, "Just let me go and I'll walk back to Bazaar. I won't say anything about you, not to anybody." Only after she'd finished speaking did she realize that she sounded like Stacy.

As though he recognized the similarity himself, Kyle chuckled, leaning toward her as he spoke. "No way. Besides, what's the difference? There's nothing to stop anyone at Bazaar who has a mind to do something fun to you—especially not now that you're practically a non-person for what you did to Stacy."

"You mean after what you helped me do to Stacy? Get a grip. Bazaar is a safe haven for me—I'm a skinslut just like them. But you." Her eyes searched Kyle's, a new coldness in her expression. "You're just a predator."

"I am." Kyle shrugged, smiling. "And that's why you don't want to cross me. Just do what I say, Erica… it'll be easier for you."

He thought she was stupid, or a pushover, or both. It really pissed her off to think that she'd spent seven whole days living with this guy before Stacy's murder—and still, somehow, he couldn't see that she was anything more than a girl. An exploitable body. A resource.

So, fine.

She'd exploit him right back.

"All right," she said, her brows knitting as though in fright and sorrow. "All right. It's just…well…" With a winsome lowering of her eyes, Erica said, "I always hoped you would be the one to do it to me, Kyle. You're not really going to just—*sell* me to some pervo snuff dealer, right? You're going to help him, at least, aren't you?"

Kyle shrugged, content to drop the act and be honest with her as long as she was being so straightforward. "Maybe. Depends on what they want. They might not even decide to kill you. I've got my own plans for you if you can make them happy enough to survive—you'll see."

"What are you talking about, Kyle?"

Kyle smiled again. His tone was warmly conversational. "Oh, sweetheart. Just a little something I do. Something to pass the time, between murders. And you know, a bit of profit."

Erica felt her cheeks flush with embarrassment as he laughed quietly. What was he talking about? Pimping her out? The idea of him doing that made her want to die. But there was nothing she could do. Not here.

Instead of fighting it, she went along with him, nodding and agreeing, trying to look and sound as much like a scared little girl as she could. Because, after all, that's what he thought of her. And it made him want her even more.

With a shy bite of her lower lip, Erica asked, "Can I have a kiss, at least, before we go? One more for the road?"

Without hesitation, he gave her one. Her eyes fluttered closed and she worked her lips apart against his. Her tongue drew back, enticing his to slide into the wet cavern of her mouth.

As soon as he took the bait, her teeth clamped sharply down upon the flesh of his tongue.

Kyle cried out with a sound of muffled agony and first tried to push her away, then realized this would result in the total loss of the organ. Instead, as her bite intensified, he grabbed her jaw, then gouged up into her eyes. Screaming in the back of her throat without opening her mouth, Erica felt the meat of his tongue start to give. No matter her own pain, she kept squeezing shut her teeth. Her hands fended off his, her knee shifting sharply down into his groin while she struggled with the wriggling fish that flapped back and forth in her coppery mouth. When his hands fell back from her face, it was only to reach for something behind his back.

Before he could liberate the gun, Erica jerked her head away and tore Kyle's tongue out from the root.

While blood poured from his mouth, Kyle produced an incoherent shout. The gun fumbled out of his hand and across the floor, and Erica would have gone after it if the resulting rattle from Kyle's jacket hadn't drawn her attention. With the bleeding muscle of his tongue still hanging from her mouth, Erica shoved a fist into Kyle's pocket and yanked out his keys before he had frame of mind to stop her.

Then, it was all adrenaline. Heart racing, limbs trembling, Erica stomped down on his groin when he made one last gurgling attempt to stop her. She spat the tongue out in his face and sprinted through the ugly old house, that hateful house, wanting nothing more to do with it.

Gunfire echoed through the first floor. She hardly recognized the sound, she was so dedicated to escape. A bullet whizzed past her left ear, but she refused to look back.

With a gasp, Erica burst out to freedom, started Kyle's car, and got the spinning wheels rolling off just as, gagging on his own blood, Kyle was very nearly within arm's reach of the trunk. His entire chin red with blood, his shirt suffused with the price of his treachery, Kyle stood behind and watched her go.

Breathless, Erica floored the gas and twisted the wheel in the direction of town.

There was only one place in the world that Erica could still call home.

08

Bazaar was packed, but as soon as Erica told the bouncer her name, she managed to get a private audience with Tania without a fuss. That should have been Erica's first clue that something was wrong.

Tania's office, though it looked like any other room at Bazaar with its sensual red draperies and dark fuchsia walls, exuded power and mystery. The lights were low. In the center of the room sat an ornate desk surrounded by green plants that seemed from some jungle. On the walls were portraits of skinsluts who had worked for Tania, stretching back long before Erica had ever come into the club.

And in the center of it all sat Tania, looking every inch the queen she was.

"I thought I told you about getting into trouble, Wayward," was all Tania said, her eyes lowered to the accounting book in which she scribbled figures verified by the calculator at her right hand.

Erica swallowed hard and said nothing, her heart racing. This was it, she realized. She knew there would be no mercy from Tania. Nonetheless, she stood before this hard-edged woman who had once been a mentor, trying to explain herself: trying to tell Tania everything that happened in order to earn a third and final chance.

"It was Kyle," Erica said, grasping for some kind of explanation. "You were right—I see what I was doing wrong, I do see it's important to go through the club for these...hobbies of mine. I've made a mistake. I've made lots of mistakes. If there's any way you could help me fix it—oh, please. I nearly died. If I had stayed with Kyle, he would have sold me to some snuff dealer friend of his." Letting her self-pity serve as the root of her method-acted grief, Erica whipped up a tear and said, "I thought he was my friend. Now I see how naive I've been. Please, give me a chance to make amends with you, Tania."

A chair scraped back along the floor; Tania rose from her seat and regarded Erica for a long moment before speaking again, her voice unnervingly gentle.

"How about Kyle? Did you kill him?"

Erica shook her head. "I hurt him, though, and he's got no car. He might die...he might choke on his own blood, for all I care."

"That's too bad...I liked the look of Kyle. He's a handsome man. It will be a shame to lose such a specimen of masculinity. Still, I'm glad you're alive. I'm sure you are, too. But what do you want me to do for you, exactly, Erica? I can't wave a magic wand and make the police stop looking for you."

Her tongue worrying against her sharp cuspid, Erica said, "I know that, but I was hoping maybe you could—I don't know. Help set me up with a friend of yours in some other town, maybe, if you know somebody who could take me in for a month or two. Or maybe you could just let me work here at the club and make enough money that I can leave town on my own."

"And you'll stay where while this happens, Erica?"

Hesitating, Erica shook her head. "I don't know," she confessed. "I don't have any friends."

Tania arched her brow. "Not one? I thought you were a college student...a pretty girl like you, no friends?"

Backed into a corner, Erica spread her hands and confessed, "I was getting along all right with my roommate in the dorms, but then that bitch slept with a boy I had my eye on...so, I set her bed on fire. Daddy had to give a lot of money convince them I was worth keeping at the school, but they decided I couldn't stay in the dorms anymore. Katrina—that was the girl—doesn't talk to me anymore." In a few seconds of genuine introspection—or what qualified as such for her—Erica suggested, "Maybe I shouldn't have set the bed on fire while she was sleeping in it."

"Erica, Erica...you are in a tough spot, aren't you? What will happen if Kyle survives long enough to catch up with you? Or what if the cops decide to come here, as they surely would? It's your own fault, of course...you should have known better than to get involved with murders outside the club. You took an unnecessary risk...but...I hate to see a girl on her own like this..."

Hope kindled in Erica's heart. With a thoughtful hum, Tania meandered around her desk and slid open a drawer. "I've been known to give a skinslut in trouble a place to stay, from time to time...but if you're going to work for me, you need to do whatever I say. And..."

Tania removed some sort of employment contract from the drawer.

"...you'll need to sign a contract, Erica."

She made a small circle around the signature line, then set the pen in the center of the table and pushed the contract forward.

Erica glanced up at Tania as she signed her name. "What does it say?"

"It says that I'll have you work here until you can leave...that I'll give you a place to stay, and food to eat. You just have to do what I tell you to do: but if you don't want to do what I tell you to do, and I've held up my end of the bargain, that means I'm entitled to force you to do what I tell you to do."

Erica looked down at the pen, at the contract with her drying signature, and finally paid attention to the contract's actual typography.

It read, in part, "I, the undersigned, agree to serve as meat in exchange for room and board."

Erica looked up in a panic, then back down at the contract. "I didn't mean to sign this, Tania—not this kind of contract. I thought—"

"What other kind of contract is there in this world?" Tania shrugged slightly, her hands spreading. "We're all agreeing to be somebody's meat for at least a little while, whatever we sign. The car loan makes you the bank's working meat; the purchase makes you the salesman's income meat. The only difference between those contracts and this contracts is, with those things, there's really no guarantee you'll be taken care of by the agreement. The car can still break down; the house could go up in flames; the employer could fold next week. But *you* know, Erica, that I'll feed you and clothe you, and even give you pleasure here in Bazaar—and that, in exchange, when I say it's time, that means it's really time. Now...is that so bad?"

Erica looked back over her shoulder at the door of the office. It had been shut to provide Erica the illusion of privacy, but she knew there were bouncers outside the door, and that one or more of them may have been listening, anyway. "Say I try to run away?"

Tania shrugged. "And go where? Are you going to sleep in the street? Going to try turning tricks until one night you meet a tongueless man who recognizes you and stabs you to death for what you did to him? Talk about karma."

She brooded over this idea while Tania strolled around the desk to drape an arm around Erica's shoulders. "Wayward, baby, it's like I told you before... sooner or later, every real skinslut realizes what she wants is not just to eat, but to be eaten. There's no death sweeter—and trust me when I say that I've seen them all. This is an honor for you! Try to view your decision with pride. You're making a sacrifice, like a fresh young girl who sells her virginity at a temple in Ancient Greece."

Hand tightening on Erica's shoulder, Tania leaned down to add in a whisper, "And anyway, what's signed is signed. This is America. Always read your contracts, baby...that's the real golden rule your daddy should have taught you."

09

By day, Erica slept in her room in the back of Bazaar: one of several double-bunk rooms that, like cells, accommodated four living bodies of girlmeat at a time. At night, when the club opened, the girls would gather to dance, drink, and fuck for customers and each other. Between customers, they spent endless conversations gossiping about who they thought would be the next one picked out to serve as somebody's meat. The walls between the sleeping bunks were painted with the Bazaar logo: an orange and white tiger face with glowing red eyes, which stared at Erica every time she walked back into the room.

When she wasn't asleep or dancing or getting fucked in various ways by a customer, Erica was serving Tania herself. Erica assumed that, since she was a flight risk, Tania wanted to keep an eye on her. The future fleshies were also given regular meals and access to showers and toilets, so Erica did not have to go very far from her quarters when she wasn't working, which was designed to minimize the temptation of escape—but then again, she had nowhere else to go. She could have tried to get away if she really felt like it, but there was only the front door of the club that led outside, and the emergency exit designed to flee the cops in the case of a raid. That led out to the parking lot, if only she could distract the bouncers hanging around it at all hours. The odds of that were slim, to say the least.

But...it wasn't so bad, was it? Wasn't Tania right? Everybody had to die some way, so Erica figured she'd might as well enjoy free food, free drinks, free sex, free drugs. She even had friends, sort of...even if all the other girlmeat wanted to talk about was either getting dicked down or who would be called out next. It wasn't a bad life, Erica guessed. It wasn't much different than what she had before, anyway. If anything, she supposed it was more honest...no more lying about being normal. No more pretending to be the good daughter of a wholesome family when all she did was think about murder. No more barely resisting the urge to drop out of school and pursue a low-paying career that didn't require higher education. She supposed, if things had turned out different, she could have learned how to be a waitress or a receptionist someday...and every time that thought crossed her mind, she decided that maybe she was better off this way, because those were, at best, dead-end jobs.

Dead-end. Erica almost laughed at the turn of phrase. She tried to, anyway. No sound came out and, strangely discouraged, she sipped the vodka tonic that now flowed for her without regard to her age.

And it was then that Tania arrived before her, a mere three months after the signing of the contract that had sold Erica's body as chattel.

"Well hello there," she said, looking down at Erica's drink with obvious disapproval. "You aren't drinking *that*, are you? I'd think even a nineteen-year-old could appreciate the finer things in life."

Erica scoffed. "Sorry, I guess I should be drinking the finest red wine with my pinkie out... What do you want, Tania?"

Tania shrugged. "What do you think I want? You've been chosen...it's time for you to serve your purpose as meat, Wayward."

Erica went a little pale in spite of the bravado she had just been exhibiting in the safety of her own head. "Already? But—but some of the other girlmeat has been here for six, seven months now!"

"It's true...but you're a hot little commodity. The boys love you; the men are willing to pay top dollar for a chance to eat you. You were born for this. They know you can handle the rough stuff. You were practicing every night with Kyle, anyway, right?" At Erica's annoyed eyeroll, Tania chuckled and winked. "Oh, don't be like that...be happy! Soon, you'll never have to worry about your old bad decisions ever again. Nothing will haunt you anymore. You get to enjoy the ultimate pleasure. The sweet release of Death."

There was something so unnatural about Tania. Naive as she'd been, Erica hadn't noticed this on her first time in Bazaar. Now, it was all she noticed. The woman exuded a certain inhumanity: as if, beneath her skin, Tania was something else. Something alien, but familiar…like something Erica had read about and forgotten when she was still a kid.

And wasn't she, really? She looked down at herself in numb incredulity while, like any good lamb offering, she was bathed before her slaughter. How strange! Erica felt so much older; at least twice as old. But Tania was right. She really was just a nineteen-year-old. That *was* forever, wasn't it? Wasn't that long enough? Enough to taste all that life had to offer, and decide it wasn't worth having?

After the attending skinsluts had bathed her—the same blonde from her initiation and Kyle's photo, she noticed—Erica was dressed in a slutty red dress and ushered out of the club through the cop exit. A weird pang came to her as she realized she wouldn't get to say her good-byes to her roommates. But, well, she supposed it didn't matter. Erica reflected as she climbed into the van that they weren't real friends, anyway.

She wondered what the others were going to think when they saw her missing. "Those dumb, crazy bitches are going to be jealous," she thought, smiling in spite of herself.

Her smile quickly faded as the van's driver put his

foot down on the gas and the vehicle shot onto the highway with such speed that it almost bucked itself out of control. Erica felt as if she were being hurled out of herself. Dissociating, she supposed. She was tossed about by the bumps, the jolts, and the sudden swerves that were all part of the excitement of the drive, but this was no amusement ride...and there would never again be anything to hold on to.

By the time she looked out the reinforced window at the back of the panel van, Bazaar was long gone: all that stood in the past was a long ribbon of endless black highway.

And all too soon, the blacker highway ahead of them gave way to dim suburban lights. She was illuminated by the glow of a few houses as they passed by; then, they rounded a curve.

In their headlights, she caught sight of what was becoming a more familiar sort of scene in those last days of her life: an old house sitting on a small rise, its yard overrun with weeds and wild grasses. As they parked before it, the front door opened and a figure in a white bathrobe stepped out onto the porch. It was impossible to make out the guy's features with the lights on behind him. She felt a pang of terror, and when he turned to wave to them, the sick sensation only deepened. It really was business as usual. So simple. Amounting to nothing.

The guy went inside and was nowhere to be found when, apparently having been advised of her flightiness, the driver of the van caught her by the arm to haul her into the house. No point in screaming...it was all legal. She had a contract.

In they went. Erica was whisked through a living room she barely saw but for gold drapes and a cigarette-burned rug. Then, before she knew it, she was down in the basement, and the van driver opened the barred door to a little room that had been partitioned off. "Whose house is this," Erica asked weakly at the familiar sight of the bloodstained, once white room that had been the setting of oh so many of Kyle's cherished snuff films.

Without answering the question, the driver shoved her inside. As the door slammed behind, Erica tripped facedown upon the darkly stained sheet of the cruelly thin little mattress lying on the floor. When she looked up and around at the disgraced room, at little flecks of gore that remained like hard onyx spines among the brown spatterings of thinner dried blood, she had to marvel.

It sure was different when it was your own death you were talking about. Oh, sure, it was lots of hot, hot fun to murder...there was power in it, or so it had seemed at the time.

Now, though...she was in this ugly, bloody little room herself. There would be no talking her way out of it. Nobody to come and save her, the way nobody came to save the girls she had seen tortured and murdered on-camera while Kyle fucked her for hours on end.

It really was kind of a fucked up, lonely feeling... but what else was new? Erica had always been a fucked up, lonely girl.

And when the door opened, she got a good sense of why that was.

Her eyes widened along with her mouth.

For just a second, there was hope.

"Dad?"

"I had a feeling...the way Tania described you, there was no chance it would be anybody else."

While he set a black bag down upon the rusty metal table fastened to the wall nearby, Erica all but rubbed her eyes in disbelief. "What are you doing here? Does Mom know you found me?"

He chuckled, unzipping the bag. "No, I haven't spoken to her yet. I don't know if I should...she's been worried sick, but I don't want her devastated by the details of this bad path you've headed down."

This was it—the lecture to end all lectures. An easy out. One long boring talking-to, then home again. Her long-lost bed again.

Her old life again.

Thank God!

"How did you know to check Bazaar's catalog? How did you know to check Bazaar, period?"

"I didn't...Tania and I go way back."

That explained all the cannibal mags the old man kept under his mattress. "Well, it's nice of her to have called you." Barely noting the camcorder he activated and then set beside the bag, Erica breathed a sigh of relief. "I appreciate her letting me go...boy, have I learned my lesson! From now on, it's Mass on Sundays and coursework every night, I promise."

"Oh! Honey." Her father uttered a dark laugh, removing a carpet hammer from the camera bag. "Can't you see? It's way too late for that."

Then he was upon her, pushing her back onto

the mattress...and the next thing she knew, her own father was straddling her waist and pulling open her blouse to reveal her tits. Erica cried out, lifting one hand only for a scream to raise from her throat as the hatchet side of the tool cleaved unmercifully into the meat of her palm. The blow left her thumb hanging by a millimeter-wide strip of gristle, and she stared at the surging blood in uncomprehending shock.

"This is such a great opportunity," said her father, laughing to himself as he raised the tool, the hammer side this time, to level the second blow. "Father/ daughter stuff is so rare in this industry because of all the consent laws. This'll be my most popular video yet. Just think, honey! All the fellas will be jerking off to your death for years. Think of all the people you'll inspire. Maybe you'll even convince a few girls to live their lives just like you've lived yours...or convince their fathers to convince them, anyway. You should be proud of yourself! You're a star."

Tears raced along her cheeks.

The hammer blows rained down.

The camera's red light and the unflinching black rings of its lens were the only witnesses for now: but Erica knew—maybe better than anyone—that wouldn't be the case forever.

OTHER WORKS
FROM PAINTED BLIND PUBLISHING

REGINA WATTS

INDUSTRIAL DIVINITY (2020)

WILD GIRL RUNNING (2020)

DOTTIE FOR YOU SEASON 1 (2021)

THE BURNINGSOUL SAGA (2021-)

I WAS AN OP DEMON LORD (2021-)

BE MY BULLY (2021)

SEDUCED BY SABINE (2021)

MAYHEM AT THE MUSEUM (2021)

IDOL (2022)

TEXAS CRUEL (2023)

M. F. SULLIVAN

DELILAH, MY WOMAN (2015)

THE LIGHTNING STENOGRAPHY DEVICE (2017)

THE DISGRACED MARTYR TRILOGY (2019-2020)

CLEAR LIGHT (2023)

ADA DART

THE RIFT BRIDE (2022-)

ABOUT THE AUTHORS

Regina Watts loves writing torrid smut, transgressive fiction, horror, fantasy, and whatever else comes to mind. Check her out on twitter (or whatever it's called by the time you're reading this) **@WritesWatts**, at her own website, or follow Painted Blind Publishing's website for more information about her work. If you enjoyed the book, don't be shy about leaving a 5-star Amazon review.

Finn Vandergrift enjoys long walks through cemeteries, collecting antique skulls, and listening to opera. He lives with his wife and one cat. When reading, his interests range from science fiction to classic literature. He hopes to one day travel to Mars. Follow him on twitter (**@eccehomoplasm8**) or subscribe to his substack for information on his newest works: **https://eccehomoplasm8.substack.com/**